A New Dawn

A Novel

Best wishes,
Sudha Balagopal

Sudha Balagopal

Laurel
Highlands
Publishing

Chapter 4: Sweet Sensation first published in *Muse India*, January-February 2014
Chapter 1: Aloneness first published in *Gravel Magazine*, February issue 2014

Cover by JosDCreations
http://JosDCreations.com

Laurel Highlands Publishing
Mount Pleasant, PA
USA
http://LaurelHighlandsPublishing.com

ISBN-13: 978-1-941087-30-5
ISBN-10: 1-941087-30-2

For my mother, storyteller

Acknowledgments

It takes a family to birth a book. A New Dawn has arrived thanks to the love and support provided by the many wonderful individuals that make up my writing family.

Thank you Irene Castellano, Publisher at Laurel Highlands Publishing, for believing in this story and for showing me how a book gets created and sent out into the world. Special thanks go to Veronica Moore, editor par excellence, for asking the right questions and for uncompromising attention to detail.

To my friends at the West Valley Writer's Critique Group, with whom I spent my Thursdays, thanks for being my guinea pigs and for helping me find my way. From the very first chapter to the last one, through several revisions, you've watched my characters grow and flourish. John Daleiden, Bob Duckles, Donna Bowring, David Wilson, Jacob Shaver, Dharma Kelleher, and all the other members, thanks for following Usha's journey with great interest. Thanks also to my earliest readers, Anna Sidak and Mikal Haaheim.

To my virtual friends at WordTango, the online writing community, I offer my gratitude. You may be spread all over the world but thanks for being there when needed, whether to rejoice at success or to lend a supportive shoulder.

To my husband, who encouraged me to write a novel years ago, thank you for that faith and much love. Much love also to my daughters for knowing that reading, and therefore writing, matters.

Table of Contents

1

Aloneness

July 7, 2012

Usha locked herself in the bathroom on a late Sunday afternoon, right after trimming a rose bush.

She hadn't watered the plant yet when a dust storm stirred up from nowhere. Monsoon season had arrived in Arizona, bringing dust—haboobs—and desert downpours. Particles whipped around, stinging her eyes. In pain, she rushed into the house, leaving the patio door wide open. She made for the powder room by the living room, the closest bathroom on the lower floor. The cool water brought some relief to her eyes. She patted her face dry with one of the towels on the rack and took a close look at her red-rimmed eyes. They didn't smart any more.

She turned the button to unlock the bathroom door and pulled on the doorknob.

The door did not open.

That was odd. She locked and unlocked the door again, then twisted the doorknob. The stubborn door stayed closed. She shook her head, shut the toilet lid, sat on it, and waited. The door might become cooperative if she allowed it time to sulk. She washed and dried her eyes again. She tried opening the door twice more. It did not budge.

An unexpected, fierce anger toward her husband, Raja, washed over her as she banged a fist on the door. How she wished she could have expressed this while he was alive. He had no business dying at the age of fifty-two, leaving her alone. If her husband were in the house, he would have heard her shouts. Instead of supporting her, he'd have been short with her. He would have expressed irritation at her ineptitude and asked why she got into such situations. He demanded excellence from himself and from his family. It got him nowhere in the end.

She looked up at the ceiling. Here she remained locked, solitary, in a tiny bathroom inside her own house. This constant sense of aloneness descended on her, enveloped her like a cloak, since Raja's death three years ago. Not trapped like this, but alone nonetheless.

Thoughtless, selfish and irresponsible of him to leave me.

When they married in a traditional Hindu wedding ceremony in India, he tied the *thali*—two, small, gold pendants strung on a yellow thread—around her neck to symbolize their union. He made unfulfilled promises. "We shall be of one mind," the vows said as they took the *saptapadi,* the seven steps around the sacred fire. "We shall remain together, inseparable."

She'd learned to live on her own in the last three years, cooking smaller meals, paying bills for the first time, and taking her car in for an oil change. She learned about investments. He hadn't told her many things.

She cursed while rattling the doorknob.

Such foolishness.

Sweat soaked her clothes. There had been no need to lock the door. She lived alone. Old habits became self-propelled. She pulled at the doorknob until her fingers hurt. The door could be misaligned. She pushed the door harder.

Panic struck.

The windowless blue bathroom, despite the comforting painting and the cheerful flower arrangement, closed in on her. The only sound she heard: her labored breath. She made a feeble attempt, "Help!" Waited. No one heard her.

This house sat on a third of an acre. The neighbor on the right had moved to Flagstaff, as he did each year, for the summer. The ones on the left took their boat to Lake Pleasant on Sundays. They would not return until late. She banged on the door with her fists. "Someone, anyone, hear this." So many walls to dampen the sound. "Someone, anyone, hear this!"

"Sell the house and move," her daughter, Veena, had said to her again two days ago.

"I don't want to," Usha had muttered without meeting her eyes.

"Why?" Veena could be relentless. "It's plain lethargy, I think. And your comfort with the familiar. Are you afraid of change?"

Usha didn't tell her she found it difficult to embrace change at forty-eight. Besides, she didn't like her daughter telling her what to do. "Please leave me alone. Stop directing my life," she said. While

Veena's suggestions might sprout from concern, Usha knew she remained an unfinished task on her daughter's checklist.

Her daughter, solemn, promised to leave her alone. "I'm just a phone call away if you need me." For the moment, at least, she took off her lawyer's hat and dropped the argument.

Tears pricked Usha's eyes.

Calm down, take deep breaths. Think. Focus on how to get out of this bathroom. Are there tools in this bathroom?

She couldn't remember. Lately, she lived in a fog. At times, she drove to work, pulled up into the parking spot with no memory of how she arrived.

The doctor had told her it would take time to recover and to adjust to life's new reality.

She examined the little shelves in the wall. Nothing there except some soap, a travel-sized tube of toothpaste, and a new toothbrush. No tools anywhere. She washed her face one more time. No new ideas arrived. She could call 911 if she had a phone, which she did not have.

She remembered a television advertisement for a medical alert bracelet. The ad showed images of women who'd fallen in bathrooms. If she had the bracelet, she could have pressed a button and help would have arrived. All the women in the advertisement were much older. She was in good health, in no danger of falling or slipping.

Veena reminded her she needed to live with people like herself. Usha couldn't imagine moving into a retirement community, certainly not yet. In happier times, Raja and she had talked about moving into a gated retirement community. He'd play golf and she'd join a book club. But that was before—well before he died—before startling truths revealed themselves, showing how those dreams would never become reality. Tears flowed from her eyes.

The damn door.

Her heart leapt when a phone rang in the house—the landline.

Will the caller wonder why I didn't answer? Will they try again?

Could be Marcy, her best friend, who'd expect her at home on a Sunday. Later, she might call her cell phone if it was urgent and leave a message.

Many families had dispensed with the landline; everyone had a cell phone now. Usha kept the old number and connection; they'd had the same number for two decades. She could never find her cell phone. When she remembered, she gave it a home in her purse. She couldn't recall when she used her cell phone last or where she placed it.

She heard the house phone trilling through the empty rooms again. "Please, wonder why I am not answering. Rescue me," she begged the unknown caller.

Veena had left town for a weekend conference in Tucson.

How long before she decides to call? How long before she comes by? She may not call until she gets home later this evening.

Over and over, Usha reminded her not to call or look at her text messages while driving.

The last time they'd talked, Usha specifically told her daughter to stay away, to give her some breathing room. By the time Veena investigated the extended silence, she might be dead.

Her breath came in rapid gasps; her lungs wanted more oxygen.

She'd shrugged off suggestions strewn in her direction by everyone: her best friend Marcy, her daughter, and her co-workers. They all said the same thing as if in collusion: three years is enough time to

mourn a death, you're too young to stay single, you need companionship, living alone is fraught with difficulty. Veena shocked her by
offering to screen applicants—as if this was a job they were applying
for—if she registered on a dating website.

Usha turned the faucet on. She let it run for a while. She
wouldn't die. There was plenty of water. No food, but certainly
water. She thought of Gandhi. He fasted for many, many days to
further his cause and lived. She might go mad in this bathroom, but
she wouldn't die.

The lock on the door remained jammed. She examined the door.
Hinges fastened the door on the right. If she managed to drive the
pins up, the door might open. She tried pulling up the pins. In
desperation, she grunted and exerted pressure. The nail on her index
finger broke. She skinned her knuckles. Her fingers became bloody
while the door remained intact.

I need tools.

She washed the blood off her hands and placed one of the towels
against the cuts to stem the flow. A nurse, long ago, told her to
remember three things—clean, compress, disinfect. She hadn't stored
any medication in this bathroom.

This would give her daughter ammunition, but she wouldn't rub it
in. That was not her style. She was an efficient multitasker, business-
like, an organizer. She pestered her mother to move on, to simplify,
and reorganize her life. When conditions changed, people must
change, too.

The phone rang in the house a third time. If it sounded like this
on weekdays when she went to work, she didn't know. She received
an occasional call on weekends. The world replete with couples and
families, their lives busy and active—the weekends especially so—had

no time for her. Three calls in a row: unusual. Usha sat on the toilet seat.

Is this one of my friends calling? Perhaps a dinner invitation? But I haven't received one in a long while.

No one came to the house unless by appointment. She grew up in India where the milkman came by at six each morning, followed by the newspaper boy, the maid, the man who picked up the trash, and even the odd neighbor who'd need a cup of sugar urgently. So much human contact in the first few hours of the day. Here, days went by without anyone coming to her door. If she didn't go to work, she wouldn't see another soul for quite a while.

A cell phone's chime. She shouted, "Where are you?" Her ears told her the instrument must be close.

She couldn't remember where she'd placed her phone after the last call. In fact, she couldn't remember the last call. She yanked open the door to the tiny wall unit again. The same bar of soap, tube of toothpaste, and toothbrush in its plastic cover stared back at her. Nothing decorated the vanity except for the flower arrangement and some liquid soap. After four rings, the instrument silenced.

She screamed, "No, no, no, don't hang up."

As if in answer to her supplication, the caller tried again.

Where in this tiny bathroom can the phone be?

She didn't find it on the floor or in the wall unit. She didn't see it on the vanity. She parted the flowers in the arrangement and sobbed when she didn't locate the phone there. Close and yet maddeningly far.

She thumped her fist on the counter and heard something jump in the cabinet beneath.

Can it be?

She kept the toilet brush and some cleaning supplies there.

She found it, her cell phone, right by the bleach. As if on dramatic cue, the phone stopped ringing. She had to have left it here yesterday when she cleaned the bathroom, having finished the call and the cleaning at the same time.

What a peculiar place to leave it.

Those numbered buttons, small as she tried to press 911. She tried three times, her fingers shook so. "Let there be enough power in the battery for just this one call," she prayed. When the call went through, the professional, impassive voice of help overwhelmed her.

"911, what's your emergency?" he asked.

"I could hug you," she told the operator, sniffled.

"How can I help?" he asked, deflecting the flow of affection.

"I'm locked in my bathroom and can't get out."

"Help is on the way. It'll only be a few minutes. Your address, Ma'am?"

She gave her address, and told them the patio door in the back was open. They wouldn't need to break down any doors. The phone in her hand served as timekeeper. In seven minutes, she heard voices outside the bathroom. "Stand back, ma'am."

They did their magic; the big, handsome guys got her out. In a surge of fondness, she offered them home-made chocolate chip cookies or mango ice cream, even coffee, tea or juice. The men did not accept the refreshments.

Alone again, she sat at her kitchen table with a mug. She doodled on a writing pad as she sipped her tea. Her injured fingers bled, reminding her. She opened the kitchen cabinet where she kept her medications and found a couple of non-stick bandages. She placed them onto her fingers. *Never lock a bathroom door again,* she inscribed on the notepad.

The house phone rang. Usha picked it up. "Are you okay? I called so many times. You didn't answer. You weren't home. Where were you?"

"Hi, Veena! I'm fine." She hoped Veena would hear the smile in her voice. "I was out grocery shopping."

"Making something special? What did you buy?" Her daughter didn't let the lie go.

"Nothing exciting. I was just restocking. So, are you driving? How many times have I told you not to call when you're driving?"

Veena ignored her. "Everything okay, though?"

"Sure. Everything's fine. Can I talk to you tomorrow? I need to shower and eat."

She didn't shower. She didn't eat. Instead, she powered up her laptop. A little voice inside her head chirped and chirped. She silenced the voice with rapid typing on her keyboard and asked Google a question. The good people there seemed to have all the answers. She typed: *Is it possible to find companionship after a loss?*

In a few seconds, she had an answer.

2

A Library Meeting

July 14, 2012

Usha arranged to meet Joel at the Central Library near downtown Phoenix on a Saturday morning at 10:00 A.M. She arrived early for the appointment; she remembered this inclination had annoyed Raja. He grumbled when she made him wait at the gate two hours before a flight. He complained when they were early for dinner parties and had to sit in the car until it was appropriate to ring the doorbell.

If Joel thought she chose a strange time and location, he hadn't said so. He asked for her cell phone number and told her he'd be there. He didn't ask any questions. She attributed it to the awkwardness of the situation.

Her tires rolled over debris. Another monsoon thunderstorm had rolled through the night before, leaving broken tree limbs and scattered garbage on the library grounds. She almost canceled, almost chickened out with the weather excuse. This morning, though, she squinted behind her sunglasses; the bright sky retained no memory of the devastating storm.

At only fifteen past nine, vehicles occupied all of the front row parking spaces. She negotiated around the trash on the north side and pulled into a sheltered spot under one of the forty-two solar wings, which spread across the lot.

She entered the library through the main doors and walked down the tunnel-like lobby. She nodded to the girls at Customer Service without throwing them her usual greeting. The glass elevators received her. She'd told Joel he could find her on the fifth floor, at a table on the north side.

The library comforted her like a second home. She loved the five-story, architectural wonder that focused on light and illusion. From the elevator, she saw reflected images in the black-bottomed pool on the first floor. Pennies glinted from the bottom of the pool, a wishing well for some. On the fifth floor, she glanced up at the floating ceiling suspended by cables over the Great Reading Room. Skylights helped light up the non-fiction collection.

She walked up to the shelves in the back—she knew exactly where the books were located—and picked up *College Essays that Make a Difference* and *The Best 373 Colleges* from the shelf.

He would find her. That was the dilemma. Her walking slowed. Dread socked her right under the ribs. A respectable, middle-aged Indian woman, a widow at that, didn't meet men in this fashion. A cultural divide yawned.

I am about to meet a virtual stranger. Virtual indeed.

The thought stopped her. On the Internet, people became their better selves. The web hid a multitude of sins and accentuated the positive. People didn't snore or burp on the Net; they exuded good cheer and bonhomie. Reality, on the other hand, had an inability to mask negatives. She'd been married for twenty-three years. She knew about reality.

She hurried back to the shelves and replaced the books. People milled around on this Saturday morning, quiet murmurs already populating the fifth floor. She'd picked the familiar library for the safety it provided. Her head bowed in thought. She decided she shouldn't be on this floor and made for the stairs.

She turned a corner and ran into a body holding a pile of hardcover books. The books clattered to the floor. One landed on her foot. She grimaced.

"Sorry, ma'am," the young man said. "Are you hurt?"

"I'm okay." She rotated her right foot, checking for injuries.

"Are you sure? Can you walk?"

"No, no, really. I'm fine." She bent down and helped him pick up his books.

"I'm sorry. Do you want me to come down with you? I can put these away in a sec."

She didn't want him to accompany her.

"I'm fine. And I'm not leaving. I was only going to get something from those shelves." She pointed to the racks on the west side.

She couldn't leave now, not while he watched her, concern written on his face. She walked back to the shelves and found her books. Her new friend waved as she passed him.

She smiled in response and made her way to a favorite table, one that overlooked the north side of the library. The words in the book blurred. She was about to meet someone after having exchanged only a couple of emails. They could have spoken on the phone and shared more information.

Her daughter didn't know about this. She couldn't. Veena liked to give instructions on clothing and deportment. She'd have asked

Usha to reinvent herself.

Usha wanted to believe finding someone went deeper than that, went beyond style and sweet talk. Beyond the superficial. A chuckle escaped.

Do I believe this?

She had not chosen her husband. She had never dated. She had only known one man for twenty-three years.

Logical and practical is how she would describe herself. Yet, she registered on the site *Begin Anew* as a reaction.

This may be a blunder.

Uncertain, she flipped through the pages of the book, forward and backward.

She distracted herself by looking at the view. Palm trees dotted the landscape. Past the parking lot below, on the other side of McDowell Road, she saw the Phoenix Art Museum. The *METRO* light rail rolled at a sedate pace on Central Avenue. In the far distance, the clear vista of mountains: evidence the storm had washed away any built-up smog.

"Excuse me?"

She heard a deep, soft, masculine voice.

Of course it will be soft. This is a library.

The awkwardness of the situation made her legs tense. She could bolt, like an unstable and unreliable person. Yet, she had asked him to meet her here. An urge to pat her hair sprouted. Strands of her shoulder-length hair tended to escape the confining clip. She smoothed her skirt down and felt her cheeks turn warm.

"Is that book about college essays worth a read?"

Her ears picked up refinement in the construction of his words.

"Oh, hi," she said.

This was the moment. She couldn't run away now. Like her, he had showed up early. She noticed he brought his own reading material. Under his left arm, he carried a couple of books. Bits of paper served as bookmarks, flagging important sections.

She had given him precise instructions: she'd be on the fifth floor, by the window, reading a book about colleges. He knew she was Indian, of medium height.

Perhaps I should have mentioned the strands of gray in my hair? All women in their forties have some gray in their hair.

The man in the grainy photo on the website didn't have a goatee.

Continue the conversation, stop swallowing. Goodness, I didn't imagine this will be so hard.

She answered his question. "Yes, it's good. That is, if you want a good essay with your college application. Did you want to see the book? Here."

"Thanks!" He took the book, but didn't look at it. "Are you thinking of entering college?"

Does he think I am a college student?

"Oh, no. I couldn't sit in a class anymore."

What should I feel? Euphoria? Excitement?

She experienced awkwardness, not connection. Once, long ago, she had experienced rapture. She married that man.

She arranged this meeting; she must go through with it.

From her seated position, she gathered an impression of height. His leanness made her think of a marathon runner. She looked up at his eyes and face: dark brown eyes, goatee, receding hairline.

My best friend, Marcy, will say he's an attractive man. She may even find him handsome.

A flash of guilt ignited.

"So tell me, did you just get here?" The words scampered out of her mouth.

A flicker of a pause. "About three minutes ago."

"Please, do sit. I'm getting a crick in my neck looking up at you."

"Sorry about that. Thank you." He sat in the chair next to her.

She took in his khaki shorts, belted at the waist and the navy t-shirt, appropriate for the forecast 108-degree day in Phoenix.

"Nice view." He stood up, looked out the window. "Great choice for a table."

"I like this table."

A cell phone rang in the library; it reminded her to turn off her own phone.

"A ringing phone in a library is not pleasant," he said.

"Excuse me, I need to…" Usha dove into her handbag. She shuffled around for a bit, and retrieved her phone from its hiding place in the bottom of her bag. She turned it off.

"I don't think those things should be allowed in classrooms, at the movies, and, of course, in libraries," he said.

"I don't use my phone much. So I don't understand people who talk or text, even when they're at restaurants or with family."

"Some people have more friends over the Internet than in real life," he continued.

He brought up the Internet. So what should I say now? That the Internet has helped me find him? He knows that already.

He interrupted her thoughts. "Does this book tell you that an essay helps to get you into college?"

Relief washed over her. This question centered on her professional strength and gave her confidence. She could stop hunting for general topics for discussion. The questionnaire on the dating website matched people based on personality and lifestyles, the qualitative yardsticks. Quantitative measures like income, education, and career took less prominence.

She described herself as someone who loved food, with a particular passion for desserts. A prospective would learn that she was a vegetarian, that she liked growing roses, that she liked hiking but hated exercise, and that she was chronically early. And of course, he'd know she was a widow.

In turn, the website matched her with a man who was long-divorced, outdoorsy, liked jazz, and liked to watch movies at home ever since streaming videos made it easy. He read how-to books and enjoyed trying out new restaurants.

"An essay is just one of the elements in an application package." *I must tone down that professional voice.* "But sometimes, a powerful essay can help push you ahead of someone else with the same credentials," she said.

"I see. You seem sure of your facts."

"It's part of my work," she said.

"You work in college admissions?"

She paused. *Perhaps it is too soon to reveal so much?*

"You could say that, yes." Averting his curiosity, she asked, "Why do you want to know about college essays?"

"That makes for a long story."

"Shhh." A student at the next table shot them an exasperated look and held a finger to his lips. His hair stuck out in different directions as if he'd run fingers through his greasy hair again and again.

The library, she realized, while safe, didn't allow for meaningful conversation without disturbing others.

"If you don't mind, I'd like to continue this discussion elsewhere. Could I interest you in a cup of coffee?" He offered her his hand. "I guess I should be more formal. RJ."

She stuck out her hand, trying to remember what Veena had told her about a handshake. *A hand-shake should be firm, sure. Not tentative.*

"Usha," she said. His calloused hand sent warmth into her nervous palm in a hold that was sure, secure.

So Joel likes to be called RJ?

Must be short for Richard Joel or Robert Joel, she decided. And he wanted to get coffee. She hadn't mentioned her inherent sense of caution in the qualitative listing on the website. That's why she'd picked the library. She would dip her toes and go no further.

"We can't talk here, but there's a coffee shop just across the street where no one will shush us." He did have a charming smile. Imperfect teeth, surprising for an American, but it made for a unique smile.

She hesitated for a second before she said, "Okay. Hold on, let me put these back on the shelf. I hate to leave books on tables, makes it hard for someone who's looking for them." If she remained adamant about staying, the student would only get more agitated.

The young man who'd crashed into her earlier waved like an old friend. She waved back, finding absurd comfort in his familiar gesture.

"Should we take the stairs?" RJ asked.

"Sure."

RJ kept an easy pace, matching her every step, never moving ahead. Her husband did not think of matching his stride to hers. It had been her task to keep pace with him. They emerged from the cool library into the scorching sunshine, blinking.

At the coffee shop's counter, she ordered the crescent-shaped, chocolate-covered biscotti and iced drinks. Hot coffee or tea didn't appeal after their searing walk across the library parking lot.

She insisted she'd pay. His face fell in dismay and he repeated his offer. She compromised and let him pay for the biscotti.

He set his drink down. "Usha. Indian isn't it?"

"Yes."

"I went to India in the early eighties with a group and had a wonderful time."

She imagined him younger, sporting long hair, traversing India with a backpack.

"Did work take you there?"

"Yes. I went on a rural education project. I came away with

17

permanent impressions of vibrant color, tantalizing spices, hospitality, and friendliness."

She liked him for saying that. He asked her a question, stopped her wandering thoughts.

"Can you tell me about the relevance of a college essay in the admissions process?"

He'd redirected their conversation away from the personal. She clutched at his question centered on her area of expertise. She bit into her biscotti and munched. "Let me ask you, if you don't mind, why you want to know. Is someone you know looking for admission to a particular college or university?"

He took a gulp from his drink and scrunched up his face.

"Too cold?" she asked, biting her lip. She had directed the conversation toward the personal.

"Yes, it hit right here," he pointed to the spot between eyebrows that showed the beginnings of gray.

"I know a trick. Try sticking your tongue to the roof of your mouth immediately. It'll help."

Surely, this can't be appropriate? There must be a handbook somewhere listing politically and socially correct areas of conversation on a first date.

She hoped her answer came across as clinical.

He took another sip and laughed. "It works, sort of. Anyway, back to your question. It's my new job, in admissions for a university. We'll have thousands of applicants to sort through."

He came to meet her, so she should make the best of it and get to know something about him.

Nebulous internal fears warned. Such warnings had not assailed her when she married Raja. She hadn't known her husband before they married. She pushed away thoughts. "So are you new to the college business?"

"No, I worked at Mile High University in Colorado before this one, but am relatively new to the admissions area. I am also new to Phoenix. So it's new job, new city, new life."

"Welcome to admissions and to Phoenix. Obviously, you'll have lots of applicants. That's exactly where the essay comes in. The scores and other numbers give you an easy way to filter applications but they don't tell you the personality of the applicant." She savored the chocolate biscotti on her tongue, trying to make it last longer.

"But what about those who have help with their applications? I've heard students hire professionals to write their essays."

"Ah! Have you considered the personal interview then?"

That crooked smile again. It lifted his cheekbones.

"It's a good idea for scholarship applicants. I don't believe we've gone that route so far." He broke off a piece of his biscotti and placed it in his mouth. "This is good stuff for a coffee shop. I bet they get it from some bakery around here." He wiped crumbs off his goatee. "You know your facts about admissions. I hope we're not rivals?"

"Not at all. I work from the other end. I help students get into colleges."

He sipped his iced tea. His brown eyes landed on her face, reading her expression. The gaze personal, though the conversation was not, made a flush splash her cheeks. He didn't look around and kept his focus on her. She glanced away, reluctant to hold the moment.

"Tell me how you find your students. Do they come to you or do you go to schools? How do you work?"

Looking down, she became aware of his little shifts in the chair, of the crossing and uncrossing of his ankles. Raja's legs had been hairier but shorter, his ankles thicker. RJ's legs, relatively less hirsute.

Why am I unsettled?

He had an attractive, low speaking voice. It made their conversation intimate.

She chided herself.

Intimate. Not an appropriate word right now.

She told him about their outreach at the beginning of each school year, about the services they offered—from coaching for the standardized tests to offering help with choosing colleges. When she finished talking, she looked at her glass. A few melting ice chips remained at the bottom.

"I'll get us a second round," he said.

While he placed their orders, Usha stared at his books on the table. The uneven scraps of paper he'd used as bookmarks bothered her. She succumbed to curiosity, opened the book about inner-city schools to a bookmarked page, and drew a deep breath. Lines highlighted in yellow jumped out at her. They stained line after line, screaming their importance. When she saw him pick up the drinks, she closed the book in a hurry.

She drained her second round of iced tea until all that remained were the ice chips at the bottom. Periodically, she gathered up biscotti crumbs with a napkin. The napkins made a little hillock on her plate.

He looked at his wrist watch. "Wow, is that the time?"

"What time is it?"

"One o'clock! This was fascinating, but I have to leave. My Internet's not working and the cable guy is supposed to come between two and four. I'd hate to miss him."

The hours had zipped by.

He rose and formally took her hand. "It was very nice to meet you, Usha. What does your name mean?" His skin felt cool, thanks to the iced tea; also, pleasantly rough as if he was used to working with his hands. She looked down at his square-tipped fingers. Her ugly, unvarnished, injured nails still bore evidence of the bathroom incident a week ago. She pulled her hand away.

"Usha means dawn."

"Usha. Appropriate." He fished in his pocket. "Here's my business card. I hope to connect again soon?"

Why did you say appropriate? Do you consider my name appropriate? Does it fit me well?

She took the card. "Glad to meet you as well, RJ," she said. He'd never know how close she'd come to leaving the library and missing meeting him. "Sorry, I don't have my card with me."

He held the café door open. She felt his hand on the small of her back, four fingertips guiding her out of the restaurant. When he released his hand, she missed the light pressure. As he said good-bye, she noticed the crooked smile again, the warmth in his brown eyes.

For all her apprehensions, the meeting had gone well—better than she could have imagined. He came across as decent, articulate, warm, focused. She considered the first date of her life a success.

She felt a shift in her heart, a move from the initial reluctance to enjoyment. His attractiveness helped. She ran over facts she'd gleaned in three hours. He'd been to India once, had moved to the Phoenix area and into his job recently. He spoke well, had a background in education, kept the company of books, had good manners. He dressed appropriately for the weather. Still something niggled.

The problem is I can't find flaws.

Granted, he'd been on best behavior. She couldn't find anything about him that annoyed.

He highlighted text books. She abhorred that. He stuck bits of paper inside books, instead of bookmarks. Not a character flaw.

He could have disagreed with her about something, some issue.

Am I missing a mannerism, a tic, a lapse in politeness?

She couldn't locate her car in the parking lot. The temperature had to be well over 100 degrees. Sweat trickled down the ridges of her spine, drenching the waistband of her skirt. Last night's storm had brought, and left, humidity in the air.

Where did I park the car?

Her head seemed to be in a fog again. The cloudiness descended when she became preoccupied with more pressing matters. The overarching thought pushed all other issues to the background.

She wiped the sweat off her forehead with the back of her hand. Only one thing she could do to find her car; it had worked before. She pushed the alarm button on her key fob. Her car responded.

Inside the car, she turned the air-conditioning to high. She dropped her bag on the passenger seat and looked at her face in the rearview mirror. Sweat shone on her forehead, and her lipstick had faded—the color probably transferred onto her glass at the coffee shop.

She had to give it to *Begin Anew*; they understood her better than she knew herself.

When she registered with them, she couldn't have imagined meeting someone like RJ. The idea tenuous, she could not have articulated what she was looking for. She liked RJ. No, she more than liked him, cultural differences notwithstanding. She liked his eyes, his voice, and his goatee.

He made her feel something she hadn't felt in a long time. More than an average sort of woman.

Dare I use the word "sexy?"

Wrapping her arms around herself in a hug, she grinned at the use of an unlikely word. She realized she still held his card in her left hand, mangled and wet from her sweaty palm. Slowly, she straightened the crushed card.

She read it.

Dr. Arjay Wheeler. Arjay. Not RJ. Not Joel. Not the man from the dating website. She didn't know Joel's last name.

Can it possibly be Wheeler? Perhaps Joel is his middle name and he is otherwise known as Arjay.

Her gut knew the explanations didn't compute.

Joel may have shown up at the library at the appointed time. She'd left by then. He probably told himself, "This lady is a flake."

She'd turned the ringer off on her phone.

She dug through her purse: two missed calls from Veena. She saw a text from Joel. "Sorry can't make it. Flat tire. Waiting, waiting for AAA. Contact u later."

She put her fingertips on her forehead and closed her eyes. What a howler. She'd just spent three hours with the wrong man.

Yet, after the initial uneasiness, Arjay made her comfortable. Everything fit right.

The thought disappeared as she heard her late husband's voice in her head: "Trust you to mess up something important."

3

Love and Marriage

December 1985

Twenty-two-year-old Usha fell in love with Raja before she met him. He had mailed her his photograph in an envelope addressed to her. Under his picture taken at the Grand Canyon, the caption read: *A true wonder of the world.* The majesty of the canyon in the picture didn't captivate her. Instead, the man in the photo took her breath away. She committed to memory the emblem on the pocket of his stylish blue shirt, the sharp crease of his gray pants, and the lazy sunglasses dangling from his right hand. The photograph stayed on her person, sometimes tucked inside her sari blouse, sometimes folded into the sleeve of her *kameez*, and sometimes hidden in the pocket of her pants.

She marked off the days on her calendar, each red cross bringing him closer. On the night of his arrival from the United States, her mother urged Usha to don a silk sari. "Raja will see you for the first time, after all," she said.

Flights from abroad landed during unearthly hours at Chennai's Meenambakkam Airport. Raja's flight, scheduled to land at 3:25 A.M., didn't prove otherwise. Her parents went to bed at 9:00 P.M., gently chiding her to get some rest until 2:00 A.M., when they would leave for the airport.

Her euphoria didn't allow for a wink of sleep. She lay restless on her bed until midnight. After, she chose a printed sari with care, picked matching jewelry, and wound a strand of fresh jasmine flowers around her single braid.

Her father drove to Raja's parents' house en route to the airport, their home five minutes away. She waited as the parents drank coffee, which she declined, tapping her feet and cracking her knuckles. Every now and then, she touched the photograph folded inside her blouse.

Mrs. Param—Raja's mother—reminded Usha, "He is simply excellent!" Usha gazed at the evidence of his excellence in the Param living room: an entire wall dedicated to academic certificates, awards, and trophies.

Mrs. Param's eyes moistened when she mentioned her twenty-eight-year-old son—an exemplary student, a dutiful, responsible son. "I could always expect the best from Raja. He didn't really want to leave us and go so far away, but we insisted. You see, the university recognized his potential and offered him a scholarship." After completing his engineering in India, he went on to study business administration at the University of Virginia, landing a job in Phoenix with his MBA. "Now that he has you, America will become a less lonely place for him," she said.

Usha's father and Mr. Param hugged and slapped each other on their backs, congratulating themselves on orchestrating a brilliant match. Colleagues at Indian Railways for over thirty years, the fathers could scarcely wait to elevate their friendship and become relatives.

The fathers discussed preparations for the wedding which would follow immediately after Raja met Usha. They had much to accomplish during Raja's three weeks in India: the wedding itself and all the paperwork so she could obtain legal entry into the United States.

Although the streets were eerily empty at three in the morning, the airport hummed with activity. The two families waited in the car until it was time to move to the gate. A throng of hundreds buzzed outside: relatives, friends, taxi drivers, and auto-rickshaw drivers.

A booming, yet distorted voice announced the arrival of the British Airways flight at 3:35 A.M. "It will take Raja time," Mrs. Param, the all-knowing one, told them. "He has to make his way through immigration, then baggage claim, and finally, customs. So, I say, at least another hour." Fifteen minutes later, Mrs. Param suggested the contrary, that they leave the car so they wouldn't miss him.

Usha recognized Raja the instant he emerged through the archway with the word "Arrivals" in big, bold letters above it. Her shaking fingers touched the photograph inside her blouse. A shiver surprised her body. She took that to be a divine sign, the connection with him palpable, immediate. Every sense in her body knew him without having met him. His parents and hers missed Raja as he surfaced in a crowd of hustling passengers pushing luggage carts. She didn't.

She couldn't stop staring at her soon-to-be husband. The gray pants, the formal black shoes, the jacket slung over his left arm, the haircut, the glasses with the thinnest of metal rims, and the wheeled suitcase he rolled behind him: everything screamed "foreign."

For an instant, she wished she didn't look so Indian in her traditional sari, then shook off the feeling. Different or not, they were affianced, this excellent man from foreign lands and her ordinary, local self.

When she turned twelve, her grandmother told her not to bother with boyfriends. They were a waste of time. Her parents would find her a prince, only the best, the likes of whom she could never hope to find on her own. She drew pictures in her head of a handsome man astride a white steed. He galloped in from exotic territories, whisked her onto his horse, and carried her away into a blissful future. Kismet played its role. Raja's name meant king. His photograph alone contracted her viscera.

He became the excellence god to her average-ness. The word "average" attached itself to Usha the moment she was born. Everyone portrayed her that way: typical, ordinary, nothing special. Neither dark complexioned nor light skinned, they described her as wheaten. Neither a genius nor a dullard, she performed reasonably well in school. She didn't grow tall, but no one could call her short either.

His mother shouted Raja's name in excitement, pushed her way through the crowd, the ever-ready tears spilling from her eyes. Every now and then, Usha wondered if Mrs. Param had aspirations to be an actress.

"*Aiyo, aiyo, kanna*! Five and a half years, five years," she said in loud, dramatic tones. "Let me look at you, my son, after so many years. Let me just look at you!"

She held on to her son, squishing him to her massive chest. Usha doubted he could breathe. Mr. Param hovered, awaiting the chance to greet his son.

Raja removed his glasses, smiled, and returned his mother's hug. Usha noticed his eyes almost disappeared when he smiled.

Can he see through those slits?

More hugs from his mother. Finally, Mr. Param got a chance to welcome him. Then, introductions. Of course, Raja said, he remembered her father from years ago. Usha shifted foot to foot, impatient and annoyed. Her father acted as if they were here so *he* could meet Raja.

"How are you? How was the flight? Jet lag will hit you soon!" her father said.

So much chatter about trivial matters.

She almost stepped forward. Decorum dictated she behave with modesty.

Should I walk up to him? Or stand, demure, by my mother? Will he recognize me from the one photograph his parents had mailed him? Will Mrs. Param thrust me forward? Or will father bring me up to meet him?

Mrs. Param made the move, said, "*Va, va!* Come, come, Raja. Meet Usha."

Raja said, "Excuse me," to her father, then walked directly up to her and held out his hand. "Hello, Usha! Thank you for coming to the airport so late at night." He took her hand between both his, covering her hand like an envelope, and there it was again, that inside contraction.

Everything and everyone faded away. Raja and she stood in a mist. If they'd been actors in a Bollywood movie, this moment cried for a song. His eyes crinkled again as he smiled.

"*As if I wouldn't have!*" she wanted to say. Instead, she settled for, "Hello, Raja! And, welcome."

The spell broke. A porter gathered luggage. Discussions followed: who would sit where in the car, now that there were six. Eventually, the two fathers sat in front, Raja and Usha book-ends in the back seat, the mothers sandwiched in the middle. No one gave her an opportunity to speak.

"Housework must be easy in America, no?" her mother asked him. "After all, you have vacuum cleaners and dishwashers and clothes washers. All the machines do your work. Here we're dependent on the moods of our maids."

"Yes, Aunty, I don't have to worry about the maid," he laughed. His chuckle made Usha's pelvis clench again. "But I do have to move the vacuum cleaner, and I still have to load and unload the washer."

As they neared his parents' place, quiet descended. They'd gone to the airport to welcome Raja. She'd met her future husband. They'd brought him home. Months of anticipation ended here.

The men unloaded Raja's bags. Mrs. Param said, "Raja should rest now, poor chap. He's had such a long journey."

Raja tapped on her window. "Give me a chance to catch up on some sleep. I'll get in touch with you later today."

Elation returned.

She liked him. The callow youths she knew from the neighborhood paled in comparison. They sent her surreptitious, but impassioned, notes through friends. Not one of them spoke to her directly. Not one of them called her on the phone. Not one of them would ask her out to a restaurant. That was not the way in their culture and in their homes.

But Raja was from America. Nothing he did would be deemed less than ideal. Her soul rejoiced.

Usha changed her clothes every couple of hours in feverish anticipation. She wore a sari first. She took it off when her mother said she didn't need to dress formally today. A skirt would be more appropriate. Her favorite peach skirt fit wrong, sat too tight around the hips. Finally, she settled on a sleeveless *salwar kameez* aiming for the casual, yet well-dressed look. She paraded in front of the mirror, walking forward and backward, turning around to check her backside to make sure the pleated *salwar* didn't billow.

When he arrived later that day, a box of chocolates in his hands, a luscious sweetness filled her mouth. She could taste the chocolate melting on her tongue.

"Hi!" He handed her the box hugged by an elaborate red bow. She studied the ribbon and wondered whether he'd tied it himself. He made no comment on her carefully chosen attire. She swallowed disappointment, held the chocolates close to her chest.

Her parents gushed, offered him coffee, tea, *dosai*. "Usha makes very good coffee," her father said.

He accepted the coffee. "Milk, no sugar."

"No sugar," Usha repeated.

"Thanks for the coffee," he said, when she brought him his beverage, his only personal comment to her.

He got down to business, spending two hours outlining the paperwork for her visa. She had her passport ready, but more work awaited, starting with passport-size photographs and copies of her birth certificate, which, he told her, the authorities required. He wrote a list. The earlier they went to the US Consulate near Gemini Circle the better. She needed proof of coursework and her marks from the university. If she wanted to attend university in the United States, she'd need those papers, too.

In a small voice, she asked, "Am I going to study?"

"You'll have to get an advanced degree to get a decent job. You see, I'm so busy, I'm not home much. It's better for you to work."

"I... hadn't thought about it," she said.

He wants me to be an independent woman?

"So responsible, so organized, he doesn't waste any time, does he?" Usha's father remarked to her mother. "No wonder the Param family is so proud of him."

Usha stared at her toes, squashing a small voice of discontent.

The next day, Mrs. Param called and invited her over. "The tailor will be here, and we need to get your measurements for blouses," she said.

Mrs. Param had picked a bright green sari with a purple border and another in gold. Not Usha's favorite colors. She feigned pleasure, smiled, and allowed the tailor and Mrs. Param to design her blouses.

Her eyes searched, but did not find Raja.

Mrs. Param interpreted Usha's restlessness and said, "Raja and his father went to choose material for a suit. We don't want men here now, do we?" Clearly, she didn't think the tailor, a man, was worthy of gender. Mrs. Param babbled on to the tailor about the wedding and the preparations.

Raja could have taken me with him. Everything does not have to be so planned, precise, and mechanical.

"You found a good girl and a good family," their tailor, an old retainer, said.

"Yes, yes, of course. You know how many cases we had to choose from?"

For a moment Usha thought Mrs. Param described legal cases. She didn't.

"We had proposals from families with daughters who are engineers, doctors, accountants. But I said there is only one criterion that is important."

"The girl must be from a good family?"

"*Aiyo*, not that, *pa*! That, of course, is a given. The most important thing for me was there should be a perfect match of horoscopes. I told everyone I would only take my personal astrologer's word for it. He said this is the best match. Usha will be lucky for Raja. And this was the only one with the perfect match. I told my son, 'This is who you will marry.' And my excellent son, he said, 'YES.'"

Mrs. Param, recovered a bundle of envelopes from a drawer, flourished it before the tailor. "My son had been much-sought-after," she said.

The tailor, one end of the measuring tape in his mouth, nodded.

Usha stood, arms akimbo, as the tailor measured the length of her sleeve. Her legs wobbled inside her *salwar*. An average girl, she'd received a bachelor's degree in economics and worked as a trainee in a bank. She could not match the standards of those girls, those cases Mrs. Param mentioned. Her father believed this match happened because he and Mr. Param worked together—and because they liked each other. In truth, this marriage would take place because an astrologer and Raja's mother said it should and because an excellent son heeded his mother's advice.

Usha supposed everyone considered her lucky.

She didn't understand why her head hurt.

The unwelcome thoughts diffused as Raja walked in, the edges of his eyes crinkling in a smile. Her pelvis did its thing again, and she berated herself for allowing doubts and reservations to crawl into her mind.

4

Sweet Sensation

June 1986

*U*sha's love affair with all things sweet began the day Raja and she had their first big clash.

The alarm woke them at 6:00 A.M. Usha made coffee and asked as she did each day, "Would you like me to pack you some lunch?" She wished she could make a substantial lunch for him, something that would sustain him through his long day. Already, she knew his answer, could predict it even: "No, thanks, *vendam*. I'll eat in the cafeteria, or go out with my colleagues."

Today he surprised her and said, "You know, Indian food has a very strong odor. I don't want the smell of spices to overwhelm the office. I'll get a sandwich as usual."

Usha's mouth fell open, words ready to trip off her tongue. She wanted to ask him why the spices that embellished her curries with a tongue-tickling zing would be considered overwhelming. His tie defied him as he tried to get the knot to sit properly.

This is hardly the time to talk about spices and their potent scent.

To combat the silence that descended after he left, or perhaps in a bid to prove her usefulness, Usha decided to focus on a special dinner. She started cooking at noon, six hours before dinnertime. Timing the call so she wouldn't disturb a meeting, she called Raja during his lunch hour.

"Yes?" he said without ceremony.

"Raja, I am planning a special dinner. Remember the bitter gourd we picked up from the Indian store last week? I am going to stuff it. My specialty."

"Okay, very good. We'll have it when I get home." The conversation lasted two minutes. Still, it was nice to hear his voice. She'd learned to tip-toe around his work and his schedules. He was a busy man.

From 5:00 P.M. on, she sat in a plastic chair on the apartment balcony and watched others return from work. The young couple in the apartment across the parking lot—about her age, she guessed—retrieved a six-pack of beer and two brown paper grocery bags from the trunk of their car. One of them dropped a giant bag of potato chips in the parking lot. They giggled. She sensed their joy. Their weekend had arrived.

When Raja hadn't returned from work by 7:30 P.M., Usha panicked and called his office. He didn't answer. She decided she'd warm the food, turned on the stove, her ear waiting for the doorbell. Raja had a unique way of announcing his arrival. At 7:45 P.M., she heard the peal, followed by the jangle of his keys in the keyhole.

He walked in tired: tie askew, the cuffs of his full-sleeved, beige shirt undone, his beard shadow appearing darker, the stubble apparent even though he'd shaved that morning.

By this time, the bitter gourd had leaked its delicious stuffing into the dish, the rice had clumped, and the *daal* had congealed. She did not smile and ask him how his day had been at work. "Raja," she said instead, "*Yenna achu?* Why didn't you call and say you'd be late? I was expecting you earlier. I told you I made a special dinner."

Her words lit a match.

"Do you realize how much stress I am under?" His voice bounced off the walls in the tiny apartment. "I have clients from out of town. Our company's business depends on them. There's a major contract on the line. Can you understand that I am working hard for us, so we can get ahead? I'm not having fun while you sit here at home."

He took off his shoes and placed them one at a time in the rack by the door.

He thinks my concern is an accusation?

An instinct to defend conquered. "I was only worried, Raja. I didn't mean to say that you're not working…."

Her heart thundered in her ears.

"The problem is you sit here all day and you have nothing to do. Show some initiative. Did you call that driving school? It's been three months since you arrived. The sooner you get your driver's license the better it will be for you."

"No. I didn't know which one to call. There are so many driving schools listed in the telephone book."

"Why didn't you say something when you called me at lunch time? You could have set up the driving lessons this afternoon."

"I didn't want to bother you."

"But you called to tell me about dinner. You could just as easily have told me you had a problem picking a driving school."

He pulled his wallet out of his pocket and placed it on the coffee table. She watched his fingers undo the buttons on his shirt.

Will he go in for a shower now and let the issue go?

He didn't. His voice rose higher. "And I'd have told you, just pick one. It really doesn't matter. Focus on the fact that you need to get independent. By the way, did you try to study for the GMAT? That test is critical for getting into business school. Did you even open the books we bought?"

"I'm sorry, sorry…" Usha's eyes watered. No one had bellowed at her like this. Somehow, the fault became hers.

How have his long hours and lack of communication become my lack of abilities?

She wished he would teach her how to drive. The notion evoked romance; she pictured close togetherness in the car. Instead, he asked her to register at a driving school. She wanted his involvement, wanted him to go with her to Canyon State University, wanted him to discuss possible degrees.

A bitter taste filled her mouth. Odd, since she hadn't even tasted the gourd dish yet. She had dropped the bitter vegetables into boiling, salted water and squeezed the harshness out of them. After slitting each gourd, she stuffed them with an onion, tamarind, and spice mix. Coating the gourds with chickpea flour paste, she deep-fried them to complete the dish.

The taste in her mouth begged to be chased away. The memory of mango *kulfi*, a frozen treat, enticed her. On Sundays, her father bought *kulfi* from a vendor who came to their door. There was no hawker here.

As Raja showered, Usha mixed the contents of a can of evaporated milk and a can of condensed milk. She blended frozen, ripe mangoes and added them to the mixture. Folding in whipped cream, she added a pinch of saffron and powdered cardamom. After whisking the *kulfi*, she poured it into an ice cube tray and set it in the freezer. Her mouth became impatient.

Raja did not comment on the bitter gourd dish or the other items she had prepared. After dinner, he checked the mail for bills and wrote checks. Between them, words remained imprisoned. A couple of colleagues called him to discuss work matters. Later, he watched what was left of *20/20* and then went to bed.

She went back to the balcony and her plastic chair. In the apartment across the way, she saw a party in progress. The young couple danced. Her ears caught strains of music over Raja's snores in the adjacent room. She ate her *kulfi* and relished the titillation of sweet mango, cardamom, and fragrant saffron. The taste allowed her to imagine she was a part of the celebration in the apartment on the other side of the parking lot.

☉☉

Raja considered life an exam in which he must excel.

He'd let go, relaxed and allowed his latent sense of joy to emerge once: during their honeymoon in Kathmandu. They'd kissed and hugged spontaneously. He'd laughed, eyes crinkling, as she tried bargaining with vendors for souvenirs and gifts for the family. They'd gone on hikes with guides and taken a boat ride on the lake in Pokhara.

She couldn't recall seeing his eyes scrunch in a smile lately. Now, they even scheduled lovemaking: Wednesday, Saturday, and perhaps Sunday. She'd learned bits of trivia about American averages from watching television; couldn't help thinking how Raja and she met the American average of twice a week.

Since she'd been married, she learned a lot about herself. She craved impulsiveness and unnecessary chitchat. She liked watching *Cheers*. She missed having friends and gossiping with them. Like any girl in her twenties, she enjoyed wandering through the mall.

Periodically, Raja asked about her GMAT preparations. She

37

didn't tell him she was not a good test-taker. Her practice tests showed abysmal results. Sometimes she resented the studying and wondered why she couldn't simply get a job.

As a first step, she needed a driver's license. She called and set up one-on-one driving classes with a private instructor. The instructor— a jovial, retired school bus driver—encouraged her, and told she drove well. After three classes, she decided to take the driving test.

The impassive examiner, a large African-American woman, made Usha nervous, and her hands fumbled on the steering wheel. Everything went well until Usha failed to parallel park as instructed.

"Please, can I try again?"

The examiner's lips lifted in a smile that did not reach her eyes.

"Honey, if you knew the number of times I've heard that. Today, you didn't pass the driving test. Practice and come back. You have to re-take the test another day."

Usha came home and flopped on the couch, cursing the blasted parallel parking. Unless she perfected it, she couldn't get her license. She didn't understand the fuss over a skill she'd never need to use. Her suburb had shopping centers with plenty of parking spaces to pull into; the apartment complex had designated parking.

A strange, bitter taste flooded her mouth. Her tongue craved something sweet. She had purchased pound cake from a nearby bakery last week. The cake needed embellishment.

She whipped up a vanilla pudding. In a large dish, she alternately layered sliced cake, instant vanilla pudding, and chopped strawberries. For decoration, she topped the dessert with slivered almonds. After wrapping the dish in plastic wrap, she put it in the fridge to chill.

Raja called to say he'd be late coming home.

It is good we had that first blowout after all.

"A group of us will be meeting to talk about investments," he said.

Grateful he didn't ask about the driving test, she used the time to compose herself.

She heard the doorbell followed by his keys in the lock at about 8:15 P.M. His eyebrows came together to create three deep furrows on his forehead.

Should I hold off on telling him about my failure? On the other hand, I have to tell him sometime. He may like it less if I wait.

"Is anything the matter?" she asked.

"No, we discussed our mutual funds. Some of them are not doing well. I should sell, I think."

"Oh no! Will it be a big loss?"

"No, don't worry, I'll take care of the finances," he said. "I have my investment group. We'll find a new strategy."

The thought of trifle pudding sustained her through dinner. She waited until he finished his dinner before she told him about her driving test. He expelled a forceful breath and visibly controlled himself by clenching his teeth, lacing his fingers together. She sat as still as a painter's model. He didn't lose his temper.

"Usha, you've got to drive to live in this country. I guess three lessons were not enough for you. Sign up for a few more. This is getting expensive."

Guilt wracked her. He'd hinted the investments were not doing okay. She had failed the driving test. She couldn't do anything right. She wished, again, he'd show her how to parallel park. It couldn't be that difficult. She'd seen teenage girls drive. Obviously, they had their licenses.

After dinner, Raja declined dessert, opened his briefcase, retrieved a newspaper that said "Investment Times," and glued his eyes on the mutual fund tables. She sat in her favorite seat on the balcony, savored every moist, delicious spoonful of her trifle pudding.

৩৩

On the day she was to take her Graduate Management Admissions Test, Raja gave her sharpened pencils he brought from work and hovered as she tarried over breakfast. He told her he didn't understand why she, always early for appointments, delayed departure for an important exam. Her mouth full, she didn't answer. She stared at his eyes and didn't find any crinkles.

When she came out of the exam, he stood outside. "How was it?" he asked. "How do you think you did?"

"Okay, but I'm exhausted." She didn't tell him she'd worried about running out of time and had hurried through some answers. Her exams in India had involved writing long, wordy essays; multiple-choice questions stymied her. Toward the end, she chose random answers in the hope of garnering a few more points.

"It was all right. I think. I hope I did okay."

"Good!"

He wanted to get some food at an Indian restaurant; she wanted to go home and sleep. They settled on take-out.

She didn't think about the exam until the score came in the mail. The envelope arrived on a Friday afternoon, giving her time to absorb the number until Raja got home. The test scores reflected her expectations. She sat on the couch, studied the number, and decided she could classify the number under average. Good enough to get into Canyon State University. Good enough for an average sort of person.

Her tongue craved something sweet to relieve her anxiety. She had a yen for *kesari*. Every Friday, her mother created the dessert as an offering at prayer time.

Usha melted butter to make ghee. In a tablespoon of homemade ghee, she pan roasted a cup of cream of wheat. She inhaled the potent fragrance. It smelled like home and comfort.

Setting the cream of wheat aside, she boiled a sugar-water mixture, adding a pinch of saffron. She turned the range off and gently folded the cream of wheat into the softly steaming water, making sure there were no lumps. Cashews and raisins, fried in more ghee and sprinkled on the *kesari,* decorated her dessert. She sprinkled powdered cardamom to finish, bent her head over the delicacy, and closed her eyes.

She didn't want an argument on a Friday, before the weekend. When he came home at 8:00 P.M., she saw his fatigue after a long week. His disheveled hair touched the collar; no time for a trim. His crumpled shirt showed sweat stains that made deep semi-circles under his arms. All this meant he wouldn't handle the news well.

She took the plunge after dinner, offering him a bowl of *kesari* with one hand, and the envelope with the other. He put dessert on the coffee table and didn't pick it up again.

He had different expectations. "Test-taking is a skill you can develop," he told her. "It's all about practice. You'll get better the more you practice. Your speed will increase and so will the accuracy."

She passed the driving test the second time around.

He turned on the television to watch *20/20.* He wasn't going to touch the *kesari.* She picked up his bowl and went to the balcony.

The neighbors in the apartment across had some friends over. On the table by their open window, she saw large platters of food.

Perhaps I can go over and say hello sometime.

They looked friendly enough.

She tasted the first spoonful.

Perfect.

She made her mother proud. Allowing the sweetness to surround her tongue, she tried to hold on to the deliciousness after she swallowed.

5

Interference

July 14, 2012

Usha needed time to recoup from the morning. Earlier, she had enjoyed iced drinks with Arjay. If the situation didn't unsettle her so, it could be called comical. She couldn't tell her daughter about the encounter in the library. Since Raja died, her daughter treated her as if she'd turned helpless, incapable, in need of protection. For the first time in her life, Usha wished for some distance from the person she loved the most.

As she drove up toward the house, she saw the sun's blinding rays reflecting off the hood of a red car parked on her driveway and murmured, "Oh dear! Did I forget she's coming?" She'd missed two calls from Veena and had intended to call her daughter back before she left the library parking lot; the intention remained just that. She gripped the steering wheel tighter.

While her lissome body spoke of her love of dance, in her looks, tall Veena shared more of her DNA with her father than with her mother. She'd shown up today with the decisiveness she'd inherited from him. Usha exhaled short, rapid breaths.

It hadn't always been this way. Until Veena went away to college, she'd been the parent, Veena the child. Somewhere along the way, the equation shifted subtly until they became equals. Then, Raja died. The relationship shifted yet again, tilted to the point where Veena behaved like the parent. Now, she couldn't shake the feeling her daughter checked on her as one would an errant youngster.

She ignored the open garage where Raja's car occupied the left side and parked instead behind Veena's vehicle on the driveway. Her daughter chose to drive a hybrid as part of the environmentally conscious generation. Many, many times she'd attempted to convince Usha to replace her car with a more fuel-efficient model.

She turned the rearview mirror and looked at her reflection. "Smile," she said aloud, coaxing the corners of her lips up into a smile. With her fingers, she lifted her eyebrows up and apart to erase any sign of a frown. Removing a tube of gloss from her purse, she painted her lips.

Her car's door grazed the spines of a prickly pear cactus. The front yard boasted a natural look, as if their house had fit itself into the desert instead of the desert fitting into the house. The two giant saguaros in the front yard, their arms indicating they sprouted fifty years ago, had become identity markers in the neighborhood: the house with two saguaros. Three ocotillos bloomed with orange flowers each spring. A palo verde tree with its green trunk shed tiny yellow flowers, making a mess of her yard. And then there were the oleanders, pink and white, a riot of color several months of the year, quiescent only in the winter. All this in stark contrast to the backyard where she'd coaxed a rose garden, proving the desert can manifest more colors than brown.

She retrieved the keys from her purse. As she inserted the key into the front door, it swung open.

"Where have you been?" Veena yelled. Her brows came together to make three furrows on her forehead, like her father's used to.

For a moment, ripples ran through Usha's body. She shook herself and decided to act normal, to be truthful. Removing her sandals by the front door, she gave her toes a wiggle, releasing tightness.

"I went to the library. How are you, dear? Come, give me a hug. I didn't know you were coming today. You know I'd never keep you waiting." She leaned forward, gave her daughter a hug, and noted how Veena held herself, wooden, unwilling to relent.

Usha walked through the cool living room into the kitchen. Veena's open laptop sat on the table. She flipped a wall switch to turn on the ceiling fan. "Didn't want the fan on?" she asked, attempting normal conversation. "How long have you been here?"

Veena followed her into the kitchen. "You went to the library on a Saturday?" Thorough, the reason the law firm employed her.

"Well, I had to meet someone." Usha placed her handbag on the table and hung her keys on the holder. Ordinary, everyday activities.

Veena said she understood when Usha asked to be left alone a few weeks ago. Now she asked questions and demanded answers. The love that motivated her hid behind unpalatable behavior.

"On a Saturday?" Veena asked again.

"I had to. What's all this about? What's with all these questions? Nice to see you by the way."

The three lines on Veena's forehead ironed themselves out. Her daughter's eyes crinkled at the corners, like Raja's.

"Oh, come on, Mother dear, I was worried. You're behaving strangely. You don't answer your phone, like ever. And now you're off to work on a Saturday. What's going on? Why didn't you call me back?"

"My ringer was off. I told you I was in the library. I checked my phone when I got into the car and I was going call you when I got home. See, there's nothing to worry about. Nothing, nothing at all. I just had things to do." Usha opened the freezer door. "Would you like some pistachio ice cream?"

Veena did not let it go. "Why don't you keep your ringer on vibrate? That way you'd know if someone was calling you. And by the way, I know you're trying to change the subject. I'm not a child, so stop trying to distract me. Sugar is bad for us, why do you tempt me like this?"

"Because, you're my daughter. You might look like your dad, but you've inherited that sweet tooth from me. Come on, have some ice cream."

Usha's phone chimed.

"Go on, get the phone," Veena said. "It's so annoying when you don't. I know that first-hand."

"That's just a text. It can't be important. You're here. No one else is important."

Veena stuck her hand inside Usha's purse, rummaged for a bit, then captured the phone. As she handed the phone, she looked at the name. "Who's Joel?"

"The person I was supposed to meet at the library." Usha placed the phone on the table.

"You didn't meet him?" Veena's expressive, dancer's eyes narrowed.

"No. He had a flat tire."

"So you went for nothing? Then why weren't you back earlier?"

"What is this? An inquisition? I told you I went to the library. I had some work. Now I'm back."

"So answer Joel's text."

"I can do that later."

"Oh, Mother! Sometimes I don't know what to do with you."

Impulsively, Usha put her arms around Veena. "Nothing. You don't have to do anything. Just stop making mountains out of mole-hills."

She put the ice cream in the microwave for ten seconds, softening it. Using a scoop, she filled two small bowls. Her omission nagged. When Veena was a teenager, Usha had told her lies tended to out themselves sooner or later. One falsehood inevitably led to another, which led to another and so on. Eventually, the liar got caught; no one could possibly keep track of a trail of untruths. Usha wondered how long before she too would be captured. But then, she hadn't lied so far. Everything she said was true.

Veena moved her laptop, clearing room on the table. She closed her eyes after the first taste of the frozen treat.

Usha asked, "Do you have plans for dinner? Why don't you stay and I'll cook something." She flinched as Veena's hand, cold from holding the ice cream bowl, touched her warm skin.

"Can we talk?"

On the surface, three innocent words. The tone not ominous nor the content. Still, those words usually meant a serious discussion would ensue. In the movies, the husband or the wife said them before announcing things weren't working out in the marriage, or to declare they'd met someone else. Usha reproached herself for being fanciful; this had to be important to her daughter. She censored disquiet and mustered a smile. "Of course. Tell me."

"You know Dad, well, he was... I miss him. You've been through a lot, but quite some time has passed since..."

"What are you trying to say?"

"Hang on. Let me say my piece. You're still young. In a few

years, I'll probably be married, perhaps even move to another state." As Usha's eyes widened, Veena hastened to reassure her. "No, I'm not saying I intend to move, I'm just saying, it could happen. And I don't like to think you'll be alone."

Usha knew what was coming. "As you can see, I'm fine. I have my job, it keeps me busy. And I have you. Of course, I have some friends, Marcy, the girls at work. But, thank you. I know you are concerned."

She stood, turned the switch to increase the fan's speed. An inside voice intoned: *tell her, tell her.* She ignored it.

"Don't you need companionship? A closeness shared with a special someone? Someone who'd be there for you?"

"Has it occurred to you that I might like being by myself?" She avoided Veena's eyes.

She'd spent the morning with a gentleman who drew her. The meeting—wholly inappropriate since it was a case of mistaken identity—left an imprint on her mind. There was nothing to tell Veena. Her conversation with Arjay had been just that, a conversation, not a date. Besides, he might be married, engaged, or otherwise committed.

"Mother, don't be angry, please. I did something for you. Remember, I did this because I love you. This doesn't mean I didn't love my father either."

The disquiet in her mind billowed.

Veena held her hand, looked into her eyes. "I registered you on a dating website: *Love After Loss.* Somehow, when I compared it to other sites, this seemed like the right one for you. So, I put in all the information as if I were you. You can log in and check it out. See who responded. Who knows, you might meet someone."

Usha jumped up. "What? What did you do?"

"I was trying to help. Don't get mad, please. I even created a new email ID so your regular email won't be bombarded with messages."

"Why, why?"

"Well, I figured, this way, you'd find someone appropriate. I know you better than you think I do."

"How could you do this? And I had no say in it? Do you realize you took away all control from my hands? I'm not sure what to say." Usha dripped ice cream on her skirt.

"Think about this seriously, please. Here's all the information you need. Please, would you check the responses?" Veena extended a lined sheet of paper toward her. It said, "Notes," on top.

Usha took the paper and rose from her chair. Unexpectedly, she found her heart hammering. She concentrated on finding focus. There were practical issues to take care of. She needed to rinse off the drops of ice cream on her skirt. The dessert pooled into a liquid at the bottom of the bowl. Her sticky fingers called for a rinse. "Not right now. Right now, I have to take care of this ice cream on my skirt." She left her bowl on the table and went toward the blue bathroom.

At the door, claustrophobia assaulted her as unwelcome memories overpowered. Illogical, but she couldn't use this bathroom anymore. She paused outside the door for a second. She decided she didn't like the color blue, either. Too depressing. She noticed the crooked handle as she pulled the door and shut it with her sticky fingers.

"The handle on the blue bathroom's door is broken. You need to fix things," Veena grumbled behind her.

"Don't use that bathroom then," Usha shouted.

She ran into the master bathroom and threw the paper labeled "Notes" into the trash bin. Closing the lid of the toilet seat, she sat on it to take several deep breaths.

Veena resembled her father, acted like her father, but had more in common with her mother than she'd ever know. If only she knew Usha had done exactly the same thing a week ago: registered on a dating website. She'd even created a new email ID for possible responses; like Veena had.

Daughters. What can one say to them?

She took off her skirt and gently washed off the drops of ice cream before hanging it to dry on the towel rod. After washing and drying her hands, she wore a different skirt.

She sat on the toilet to think.

In a couple of minutes, she answered Joel's text.

6

An Allergic Date

July 21, 2012

sha took the Crystal Canyon—the aptly named glass elevator at the Central Library—up to the fifth floor where she experienced an odd sense of déjà vu. Her wristwatch showed 9:30 A.M. As habit dictated, she arrived early. She'd asked Joel to meet her at 10:00 A.M. Stepping out of the elevator, she hesitated, then shrugged. Last week this time, she met Arjay here. Unlikely she'd see him again.

The dating website *Begin Anew* chose Joel as her best match. As match-making professionals, Usha believed, they must know a great deal about linking profiles. She combed through their suggested list of five several times last week. The site ranked responses, indicating Joel was the ideal fit. She had exchanged a few emails and texts with him, mostly pertaining to scheduling and rescheduling a meeting.

Easier to get to know someone in person.

Sometimes, a nebulous, innate sense, not quite linked to plain old logic, told her things her head could not. Her presentiment now told her to leave, to press the "Down" button on the panel outside the elevator's door. Some people called it woman's intuition, others a gut-feeling. She ignored the fingers of apprehension raking her belly.

Her logic or that which came from the brain was what mattered, Raja had said often. He would have asked her to handle this like he would one of his projects: set goals and timelines, plan on going from initiation to development, then production, or in this case, execution; remember to set controls for monitoring, altering strategy, timelines or even methodology, depending on roadblocks that threatened to derail the project. Ultimately, the goal, that end which one hoped to achieve, should reign supreme.

Good words. This is my life, though, not a project.

She walked through the aisle on the left side, toward the windows. Saturday mornings tended to be less crowded. This morning, a bald, heavy-set man occupied her favorite seat. She cast about for another chair and found one between a young man buried in his computer on the left, and two older ladies on the right. Joel hadn't arrived yet.

She walked back to the stacks and picked up *College Essays That Make a Difference*. Still twenty minutes to go before Joel arrived. After hanging her purse on the chair's back, she opened the book to the last page, then flipped the pages backwards. Last Saturday, Arjay had asked, "Is that book about college essays worth a read?"

Somebody had a cold. *Sniffle, sniffle.* Usha turned her head. The bald man. He had his eyes closed in preparation for a sneeze, breathing heavily. It came soon enough: loud, explosive, shattering the quiet on the fifth floor. Again, *sniffle, sniffle.* Usha turned away, lest she be caught staring.

A sneeze should be a private affair.

Another loud sneeze exploded, followed by a cough. Every head in the vicinity turned, looking at the man caught in a sneezing paroxysm.

She tried to get back to her book. Last week, Arjay and she had decided libraries ought to ban cell phones. She smiled.

How can one ban a sneeze?

A momentary lull ensued.

"Are you Ah-sha?" He pronounced her name wrong.

The bald man with the awful cold stood before her.

"Joel?" She attempted to hide confusion. "It's pronounced Oosha," she said. Joel's image on the website showed him with hair on his head, clearly an old photograph.

"Yes! Yes! Glad to meet you, finally!" He extended his right hand. In his left, he held a few balled-up tissues. She looked at them, hesitated, and wondered if she could refuse a handshake.

It should be up to him; he should apologize for his cold and keep his hand to himself. She bit her lip, praying the germs wouldn't transfer.

He took her hand in a tight grip, pumped it up and down with much enthusiasm, until he saw her grimace in pain. "Sorry! Sorry!" He pulled out a chair and sat down. "I hope I didn't hurt you. I got here early, got here early."

Usha opened her mouth. Before she could say something, Joel went on.

"My allergies kept me up last night. But this time, I wanted to be early. No missing this appointment, you hear, no missing this appointment."

Already his repetitions had begun to annoy. Usha inhaled. Her inner sense had warned her.

She chided herself. Her principles dictated she should not judge people on superficialities. Mentally, she ran over his attributes as listed on the website: outdoorsy, liked jazz, liked to watch movies at home, read biographies, enjoyed restaurants. And, he'd been divorced for a long time.

Outdoorsy. He didn't dress like someone who hiked or ran. Even if he did run—and she shouldn't judge him by his size—his allergies would not allow him to be outdoors.

"Nice to meet you, too, Joel."

"Can you believe what happened last week with my tire? Too bad. Too bad. Still, I'm here now, with my nasty allergies!"

Have to keep the conversation going.

"Your profile said you were outdoorsy. Do you like to hike?"

"No, no." He laughed; it caused him to cough. She waited for the spasm to pass. "Do I look like I like hiking up Camelback Mountain? I meant I like picnics, I like eating outdoors. I like eating outdoors. I like restaurants that have patio areas where you can people watch, people watch as you eat."

Usha stared at him with narrowed eyes. *Guess that's a new definition of outdoorsy.*

He squeezed his eyes shut again. She braced herself for another big one. His sneeze unleashed itself, bursting like a mini-bomb on the fifth floor of the library. More heads turned, seeking the source of the explosion. Her hands covering her mouth, she cringed and looked away from Joel toward the racks on the left.

It can't be.

Arjay stood in front of a shelf, running his hand across some books, clearly looking for a particular number or title. She turned her head away from him, facing Joel.

Perhaps from the back, he won't recognize me.

Arjay had no way of knowing she had mistaken him for someone else, particularly a date. Last week, they'd had a formal, civil discussion about colleges, as acquaintances.

If he walked over to greet her, she'd have to introduce Joel. How would she present him? As a friend? Then, what would Arjay's opinion be of her choice of friends? Did it matter?

Joel recovered. "Sorry, Sorry," he said. "I need to reorder my medication. It's not usually this bad in the summer. In the spring, in the spring, yes, yes."

Usha looked down at her feet and hoped Arjay had moved away.

"You see, I never had allergies until I moved to Arizona. Anyway, let me tell you about my business," Joel went on. "I run a chain of car washes. Very successful, very successful. I work seven days a week, seven days to keep a tight rein on the business. Have to, have to, these days. What do you do?"

"Oh, I help kids get into college."

"And?" Joel didn't seem too impressed.

Perhaps he isn't a proponent of higher education

"It's very rewarding. Particularly if these kids come from families where neither the mother nor the father have been to college. It uplifts the family."

"Oh, okay."

Usha heard his lackluster response followed by a strange rumble. For a moment, she thought the sound came from him.

Her handbag shook, swaying against the back of her chair. "Excuse me!" she said before she opened her bag.

Where in this mess is my phone hidden?

Veena organized her purse in compartments with a slot for her phone, a pocket for her change, and another for her make-up. Usha, on the other hand, preferred a capacious bag into which she threw her keys, credit cards, cash, receipts, loose change, a stick of gloss, and a seldom-used handkerchief—her daughter had embroidered the fabric when she was in middle school—without organization. She stuck her hand into her bag now, frantically rummaging for her phone. The phone stopped vibrating. She found it entangled in the handkerchief.

Bless you, Marcy!

She'd met Marcy, a neighbor in their apartment complex, a few months after she'd come to the United States. Her friend had moved away to California after an acrimonious divorce, called often, and visited every now and then. Overwhelming gratitude swept through her. Marcy gave her the perfect opportunity.

"Joel, I hate to do this, but this is a very important call. I have to call back. If I don't come back here it's because I had to leave."

Joel didn't look disappointed. "No problem. I can call you later and maybe we could do one of those patio dinners I like when I'm feeling better?"

"That would be nice." Usha disliked the lie. "Excuse me, and I'm so sorry!"

She grabbed her purse and rushed toward the stairs, as if chased by a dog. "Collect yourself," she muttered under her breath. She decided to put him off if he did call. Nothing could induce her to endure another minute with that man.

Joel called behind her in his nasal tone, "Nice to meet you, by the way!"

She needed a hideout. Her office, where she could seclude herself and reflect, beckoned. She could not tolerate running into Joel in the parking lot.

Or worse, Arjay.

Face flaming, she raced down to the second floor, taking brisk steps toward the south end of the floor. An unlit sign at the top of the glass door read, "Campus Station." Retrieving the keys from her purse, she let herself in, switched on the lights, and locked the door behind her.

Inside her office—located on the left, past the reception area—she placed her handbag and phone on the table, and realized she still had the book on college essays with her. Before she left the library, she needed to return it to the shelves. First things first. She pumped a generous amount of hand sanitizer from the bottle on her desk and rubbed her hands.

Can I apply the sanitizer all over my body?

A nervous laugh surfaced. He'd only shaken her hand.

A knock on the door. "Oh, go away!" she hissed. She didn't want to open the main door, not when she was by herself. A smile broke out. Campus Station, located on the second floor of this library, could hardly be unsafe. Someone believed they were open today. A sign by the front door clearly displayed their hours: Monday through Friday—10:00 A.M. to 12:00 P.M., 1:00 P.M. to 5:00 P.M. The visitor, or visitors, would read that. They'd leave soon enough.

A couple of minutes later, she heard another series of rapid little knocks. *Rat-a-tat-a-rat-a-tat-a-tat.* A pause, then repeat. Annoyed, she decided to open the door to tell the visitor that they would open at 10:00 A.M. on Monday morning.

Through the frosted glass door, she saw the figure of a man. She opened the door and gasped.

"Arjay?"

7

A Perfect Gentleman

July 21, 2012

rjay? Arjay?" Usha knew she came off a little deficient. Her hand flew to her heart, as if to calm it down.

No need to be embarrassed.

"Yes. Hi! Sorry, didn't mean to scare you!"

"How did you know I'd be here?" She realized she'd made a premature assumption. "Perhaps you didn't?"

"I thought I saw you upstairs. On my way down, when I saw the office lights, I decided to check."

Did he see me with Joel? "Oh! But…"

He must have known what she was going to say since he pointed to her name on the plaque outside, right beside the word: *Director.* "How many Ushas could there be in the college admissions business?"

He smiled his crooked smile. The only man she knew who could flash a charming smile with uneven teeth. He made her want to smooth down her hair, apply a fresh coat of lip gloss, and brighten her eyes with mascara. She should invite him in and tether her wandering mind. He awaited her answer.

"Yes, of course. That's logical."

"I wanted to ask you something. May I come in?"

"Yes, yes. Do come in." She opened the door wider, allowing him in before shutting the door. "Technically, we're closed today," she said.

She led the way inside, grateful he walked behind her. She blinked several times to shake off a rivulet of nervousness.

Be calm and poised.

In her office, she gestured to a chair in front of the desk, "Please, sit down." She walked over to her chair and said, "What is it you wanted to talk to me about?"

Am I too business-like? What are the current rules about talking to a man?

He brushed his knuckles against the goatee.

Would that feel rough? Stop it!

"Before we start... So, you know about me?"

That's a strange question.

He'd told her about his job, in admissions at a local university, last week.

"Yes, of course."

"Good." His shoulders sagged in relief. "I'm new at this... whole thing."

"I understand." He had new assignment in an unfamiliar city. "It can be daunting."

He expelled a breath. "Good."

Moments passed.

Say something!

"Would you like some water?" she asked.

"Sure, thanks."

Ordinary, everyday words from the English language bounced between them. Yet feelings, impressions, and sensations piggybacked on those words as they gamboled back and forth. Her ears picked up the shuffle of his feet as he readjusted himself, her nose caught an emanation of woodsy aftershave, and her eyes, on his chest, observed its rise and fall with his breath.

Glad to have something to do, she walked out of her office to the refrigerator in the meeting area at the very back. She extricated two bottles from a case, and, wrapped her hands around the cold containers, willing them to calm her. When she returned, she found Arjay outside her office, staring at posters on a wall.

The common area by the reception displayed posters and brochures from universities all over the world.

"Colleges send us promotional material all the time." She handed him a bottle.

He nodded, drank half the contents in one swallow, and walked over to a table displaying information on scholarships and financial aid packages.

"I can see you've worked on this enterprise," he said. "Nice job!"

"Thank you."

Back in her office, he placed his water on the table. Last week, he had appeared confident, more forthcoming. Now, he measured the words before he spoke them, they emerged slower and more deliberate.

"I've been thinking about our conversation last Saturday," he said. "I liked that coffee shop."

Her heart danced a quickstep inside her chest. *He'd thought about her!*

He was not her date; never was. She gulped.

"I'm glad. I liked the coffee shop, too."

He didn't say anything.

"What is the name of your university?"

"I came to this office once before. I was in the library, browsing, and I found Campus Station. I didn't get to meet anyone, though. Apparently, I have to get in line?"

He hadn't answered her question.

"No, it's not that hard. Afternoons get busy and we have a small staff, but we're always willing to talk."

"I see you have access to students." He gestured to the large notice board outside. It displayed information on classes for the college entrance exams. "You can influence their choice of universities." He drummed his fingers on the table. "I think I have a plan that might be mutually beneficial. You want to send students to a university. I want students to come to ours."

So it really is business, after all? Disappointment squeezed her heart.

"Okay, so where's this idea going?"

"Here's my plan. If you could get a group of high school students in their junior year, say, and convince them to spend a day with us on campus, we'll do our best to woo them. We can come up with attractive scholarships, aid packages, or whatever it takes."

"What's the name of your university?" she asked again.

"Valley University."

"Ah, I see. Aren't the local students deluged with mail from you? You're already doing the necessary things."

"But you, Usha, you represent Campus Station and you come with a certain credibility."

"Arjay," she liked the sound of his name, simple, yet unusual. "Arjay," she said again. "We don't represent any particular university. All we do is urge kids to apply, help them find the school that fits them best, and help them with the application forms. Often, they pick our local public universities. If your school is a fit for someone, of course, I would urge them to apply there as well."

He brushed his knuckles against his goatee again. She'd begun to recognize some of his gestures. He's thinking, she decided. A few gray hairs added extra dimension to his beard. The graying hair and the lines on his forehead gave his years away despite his fit body. She guessed he'd be fifty or thereabouts.

"I understand. But it would be great if you could help Valley University with outreach. There's got to be a way for us to work together."

He wants to work together. Why? What is he looking for?

"I have a question," he continued. "If students can access you for free, how do you operate? I mean where is the money coming from?"

"We work with local businesses and big corporations. They make this happen."

"Ah... I see. They benefit in turn, when they hire qualified graduates to staff their company's needs!"

"I'd like to think it's their community spirit," she said. "The library itself, you realize, is free for everyone, and, like the library, we want to be this resource for anyone wanting to go to college."

He leaned forward.

This close she could see the lines on his forehead.

"So, Usha, how can we work together? I believe we have a synchrony in our ideas."

Her office had never felt so intimate.

He wants to keep in touch. One small move of my hand and I can feel the warmth of his skin. Don't!

"Arjay, I'm sure we can work something out within our boundaries here."

"May I have your card?" He picked up a business card from the stack on her desk and studied it. "I'll email you some thoughts. Will you respond?"

When he extended his hand, she took it, moist from the condensation on his water bottle. "Certainly. I'll look forward to your thoughts."

His eyes rested on her hand in his. She didn't pull her hand away.

"If you're also leaving, I'll wait till you lock up."

What a gentleman.

She slid her hand out of his, picked up their empty plastic bottles, and dropped them in a bin labeled *Recycle.*

The book on college essays on her table caught her eye as she grabbed her bag. "Gosh. I forgot. I have to go upstairs, put this book back." She lifted the book, then replaced it. "Never mind. I'll return it later."

They walked downstairs in silence.

Outside, he said, "Good-bye, then. You don't mind meeting with me again, do you?"

"Of course not." She couldn't stop the grin that escaped.

"I look forward to it. And would you think about what I said?" He looked at her, a question in his eyes.

"Yes, I will."

When she got into her car, she realized she hadn't spared a thought for Joel since leaving him stranded on the fifth floor.

Raja's project plan had gone awry.

She'd run into Arjay instead: her mistaken date.

"When are you going to learn to follow through on your plans?" Raja's voice asked.

For a split second, guilt washed over her. Then, she shrugged. "This isn't your plan, it's mine. So I can change it when I want to," she muttered.

The cell phone buzzed into her reverie. Perplexed, she scratched her forehead.

How on earth did the phone end up in the passenger seat?

Usha picked up the phone and said, "Hello?"

"Why don't you ever answer?" said Marcy.

She forgave the indignation from her best friend.

"Sorry, Marcy, I'm so sorry. I should have returned your call." Usha knew how to sidetrack. "I had a date and I couldn't answer."

"Date! Date! You had a date?"

8

A New Friend

October 1986

Every evening, Usha sat on the white plastic chair in their east-facing balcony. Her favorite part of the apartment, the balcony offered refuge, comfort, and a release from the clutches of claustrophobia. Today, a novel on the floor by her chair couldn't hold her attention. The mug of herbal tea she held cooled as worried thoughts heated her head.

She'd hurled her breakfast the past two mornings. Aromas she ordinarily loved made her nauseated. She scrubbed and scrubbed her kitchen sink, the stovetop, and all her pots and pans. The sugary, saffron laden scent of the *gulab jamuns* she'd prepared two days ago lingered. Unable to scour the smell of the dessert, she almost trashed the sugar-soaked golden dumplings.

Exhausted, she couldn't focus on homework. Assignment deadlines loomed even as a desire to curl up into a ball and sleep besieged.

She drove herself to the doctor's office after class. Once before, Raja had taken her to see the doctor for the stomach flu. Instead of medicines, this time the physician offered congratulations. The doctor raised an eyebrow when Usha didn't appear ecstatic.

A deep, belly-level ache made her want to cry. She stood, placing her elbows on the railing, her palms around the mug.

A baby will arrive in seven months, May 1987, only sixteen months into my marriage.

A car horn jolted her. She dropped the mug of tea onto the walkway below. When she saw the ceramic shards on the ground, tears that had hovered all day pricked, demanding release.

"Hey! I'm sorry." The young lady who lived in the apartment across from theirs called out from the parking lot below. Her high pony tail bobbed as she shook her head. "It's my fault. I was trying to get your attention to say hello!"

Usha didn't see the neighbor's husband today. For weeks now, Usha had watched the couple. They went for intimate walks: her arm across his back, fingers tucked into his back pocket, his arm around her waist. They walked in unison, reminding her of the three-legged races at her school's sports day. From the open windows of their apartment, she heard music on Friday evenings, the dining table laden with goodies visible from her seat on the balcony.

Usha grabbed a broom and dustpan, and hurried down the stairs.

The young lady with apologetic hazel eyes ran up to her. "This is my fault. Let me sweep this up. I'll get you a new mug." She stuck out a hand. "By the way, I'm Marcy. What's your name?"

"Usha." The idea of receiving a replacement mug embarrassed her. "Don't worry. It's just a mug. I should have held on to it."

"Oosha, I love your Indian accent! I work at a Montessori school where we get many Indian children," she said.

Usha looked at Marcy's formal skirt and silk blouse.

"Give me the broom. And that's an order," Marcy said.

"But your outfit…"

Marcy did not answer. She took the broom from Usha's hands, and swept the shards into the dustpan. "I guess the drink will evaporate."

She stopped as if a thought had come to her. "Would you like to come over for a cup of coffee? Larry is out with his friends."

Usha hesitated. "Um… I have to take this upstairs," she pointed to the broom and dustpan.

"I'll take care of the trash. It's the least I can do," Marcy said.

"But…"

"It's just coffee. Are you expecting your husband back soon?"

"No."

"Okay. So, that settles it."

Usha's head throbbed. "I'm not sure I can drink coffee. You see… you see, I'm pregnant."

There, I've made the declaration.

"Congratulations!" Marcy stared at her. "Come on," she said, "I'm sure I can get you some orange juice or something."

Marcy's untidy apartment welcomed with its cheerfulness. A pink throw on the worn couch spoke of intimacy. Usha supposed the couple watched television together under the shared blanket. Newspapers and magazines strewn across the coffee table talked of hurried reading with breakfast. Empty coffee cups served double duty as paperweights.

"Make yourself comfortable. Sit anywhere." Marcy removed her jacket and threw it over the back of a chair. Usha chose to sit at the dining table. Marcy placed a glass of orange juice in front of her. "I think crackers would go well with that."

"Thank you, but no crackers. This is good." Usha sipped her orange juice. She felt its cold trail down her throat.

It won't do to feel sick now.

She placed a hand over her mouth.

Marcy settled down next to Usha with her coffee. "So, exciting news, huh?"

Usha attempted a smile. The coffee's aroma bothered her. "I suppose so."

Marcy studied her as if weighing her response. She cocked her head to one side, and scratched her right ear. "Pardon me for saying this, but you don't sound too enthusiastic."

Usha wished she could retract her tepid response. She'd shared personal news with someone she met fifteen minutes ago.

My doubts and inner turmoil should be private and shared only with my mother or with someone as close.

She attempted salvage. "It's just that the timing's not right."

"Hey, it's never the right time. It'll be great! You'll see."

Everyone in this country seemed to possess a positive attitude. She wished she could imbibe some of that energy.

"I hope so. Everything's complicated. I came from India a few months ago. We're getting used to being married. I got my driver's license a month ago and driving is new to me.

"Also, I'm enrolled in an MBA program. This is my first semester. And... this pregnancy throws everything off."

"Plans get broken. You make new ones."

"I'm not sure what my husband will say."

"It's his baby, he'll be delighted."

"I hope so. But, Raja, he likes his life organized. The idea was for me to finish my MBA, to get a job. Then, we would buy a house, move out of this apartment, get a second car, and then have the baby. In three years. So now, everything changes."

Why the disloyalty? I shouldn't be talking about Raja with someone I've just met. We've created this baby together, so I should tell him the news before anyone else.

He liked order, though, and their lives were about to be disordered. With three in the family, he would say they needed a larger place than their one bedroom apartment. The pregnancy thwarted his plans for her education.

She couldn't stop feeling guilty as if she alone had caused this turbulence.

"Life is full of the unexpected. Embrace your pregnancy." Marcy patted her hand.

Best not to think until the queasiness settled and the pounding in her head eased.

Something salty may be a good idea.

"Marcy, I think I'd like to try some crackers," Usha said.

Marcy placed a few crackers on a plate. Usha nibbled on the edge of one, hesitant to take a larger bite.

"Okay?" Marcy said.

Usha swallowed some orange juice to help ease the bulge in her throat. Kindness made her susceptible to tears.

Marcy patted her hand again. Her voice became husky. "I'd like to say something, if you don't mind. Enjoy your blessing."

Usha nodded.

She knew her nod lacked conviction when Marcy went on to say, "Larry and I had been trying to have a baby for a while. And finally, after many, many tests, the doctors told me I could never ever have one."

At that moment, Usha knew they'd be the closest of friends.

9

Sweets for Sweet News

September 1986

A t dinner, Usha pushed the food around on her plate as she mulled over her idea. She got the notion from a ritual she saw in her family, a practice overly dramatized in Indian movies. "Good news! *Moo meetha karo.*" Sweeten your mouth. Good news accompanied by treats became that much sweeter. In the movies, the heroine would place a bit of dessert or a delectable treat in the hero's mouth while gazing coyly at him. After the very first bite, he'd understand the nature of the communication and jump up and down in delight. While Usha did not expect quite such a reaction from Raja, she hoped her action would hint at joyful tidings.

Good thing I didn't dump the sugary gulab jamuns *into the trash.*

Raja, preoccupied through dinner, didn't observe how little she ate. After he finished, he retrieved a folder from his briefcase and

69

buried himself in the numbers on a chart. She noticed that the gray shadow under his eyes had darkened to black this Friday evening; the color told her he'd endured a long, tiring week.

The fragrance of saffron from the *gulab jamuns* made Usha uncomfortable. "Not now, not now," she muttered and placed two *jamuns* in a dessert bowl.

Ridiculous how nervous I feel. It shouldn't be this way between husbands and wives.

Altogether too serious, too organized, too planned, he made sure his life went according to his blueprint. This event veered them from the chosen path. She had considered giving him the news over the phone so she could become a disembodied voice bearing not-so-welcome news, offering him time to absorb the new reality. She had not called him from the doctor's office.

She stole a look at Raja, toying with the idea of postponement, tempted to wait so he could enjoy a restful weekend. If she waited until Monday, though, he would know she'd kept the news to herself for three whole days. Raja had his feet on the coffee table as he studied some graphs. Every now and then, he removed his glasses, tapped the edge of the frame against his teeth, and nudged thoughts along.

Tell him the news now; get it over and done with.

"Here, open your mouth," she said, scooping half a *gulab jamun* into the spoon.

"What? You're going to feed me?" Raja swung his feet to the floor and placed the graphs on the coffee table.

Not equipped to imagine this could be a gesture of affection, he didn't play along. "I'm not so busy that I can't feed myself, *kudu*," he said, the beginning of a smile crinkling the edges of his eyes.

She latched onto the hope at which his smile hinted. "No. Let me do this, I insist." She placed the *gulab jamun* in his mouth.

"Sweets for sweet news," she said, remembering her new friend Marcy's infectious energy.

"What sweet news?"

"I'm pregnant." She intended to start with a preamble, but lost her prepared words along with her confidence.

Raja rustled his papers and reordered them.

Her ears picked up everything but what she wanted to hear. She'd always imagined silence to be an absence of sound. It proved otherwise. She heard sounds, magnified: a car pulling over in the parking lot, a neighbor's television emitting canned laughter, the air-conditioner powering on, the leaky kitchen faucet dripping.

Say something.

"Raja," she said, "was the *gulab jamun* good? Maybe I can get you more?" Her questions resonated, incongruous to her ears.

Raja shook his head. The crinkles disappeared from the edges of his eyes. He took the bowl from her hands, finished the dessert, and rose to place the bowl back in the sink. His actions rolled along in excruciating slow motion.

She hurried into the kitchen. The *gulab jamuns* needed to go back into the refrigerator.

The strong, sugary aroma wafted up to her nostrils and sent an immediate reaction to her belly.

Oh no, not now.

She charged into the bathroom and closed the door. As she bent over the toilet, she pictured Raja back with his papers. Her stomach cramped. She brought up her meager dinner, tears sliding down her cheeks.

She saw him outside the bathroom door when she came out—her mouth clean, face washed. He placed a gentle hand on her back.

A wan smile surfaced when she saw the worry written on his face. He handled projects in crisis at work. But he did not know how to

71

handle physiological problems.

Perhaps the nausea plaguing me is a good thing, perhaps it came at the right time.

"Are you okay? That didn't sound good. Did you go to the doctor?" he asked.

"Yes, I did. I went this afternoon. That's where I found out."

"I suppose this was what the illness was about the last few days?"

She nodded, poured herself a glass of water.

"Well," he paused. He had absorbed the surprise. She could almost see his brain ticking, working, ideas running hither and thither. He stood straighter. "This throws everything off. We have to find a house and move before the baby arrives. I have to rearrange the investments. We have to see about your university schedule."

She wanted to say, *"No, we don't have to. We don't have to move. A baby needs very little room. The schooling can be postponed. And can you stop planning for now and simply enjoy the news?"* She didn't.

A burp let loose.

He knew how to handle this. He handled bigger crises at work, complex projects that veered away from project plans. If she emphasized the wonderful nature of the news, he would make accommodations.

He sat down on the sofa and placed his feet on the coffee table. He removed his glasses and tapped the edge of the frame against his teeth.

He didn't jump up and down like a movie hero. He didn't hug her and declare, "What a gift, what a gift from the gods!" Instead, he reflected, prepared, and sketched. That was his way of welcoming an addition, changing his path.

His thoughts didn't allow emotions to lead. He went into his deliberation mode. "I should say congratulations. So, congratulations.

To us. I suppose we should call home, tell everyone the news?" he asked.

His logic provided the suggestion she needed. Their families of-fered what she craved, words brimming with enthusiasm. Everyone gushed in delight. Advice overflowed through the phone line: eat well, get plenty of rest, listen to good music, and don't watch horror movies. Over the phone line, the elders bandied baby names about, for both boys and girls.

After they hung up, she noticed she'd begun to feel better. She rubbed her lower belly. That cold, sick feeling at the pit of her stomach had disappeared.

I think I'm ready to eat some gulab jamun *now.*

10

Wonder Baby

May 1987

Usha thanked baby Veena for arriving into this world on a perfect spring morning in May, the Saturday before Memorial Day holiday. Marcy stood by, ready to drive her to the hospital if Raja could not. But, as it turned out, Veena timed everything just right; she appeared four hours after Usha's water broke at 5:30 A.M. on Saturday.

Raja thanked Veena, too. He didn't need to take extra days off, he could return to work on Tuesday morning without missing a single day.

Usha called Veena her wonder baby for making Raja fall in love with her. He held the swaddled baby as if memorizing her every feature: her toes, her fingers, her nostrils, her quivering lower lip. He became besotted with Veena; not with her soft black hair or her long lashes, nor with her dimpled hands or the round cheeks. He didn't admire the power in her little lungs when she belted out one of her screams nor did he marvel at her contemplative gaze. Instead, he told Usha, "This baby is amazing. Baby Veena knows the value of organization and the power of optimization. Look at when she came into this world. I know she is destined for great things."

Marcy and Larry visited immediately. They oohed and aahed over the baby.

Marcy said, "Oh, you're a cutie, aren't you?"

Larry told her, "You are a good baby. Yes, you are."

Raja on the other hand, conducted serious conversations with her; he believed she listened even with her eyes tightly shut. He held tiny Veena in his arms in the hospital, told her she must set great goals for herself; she must reach for a doctorate from no less than an Ivy League school.

"We bought this house since we knew you were coming. I know I did the right thing even if it stretches the finances right now. I'll send you to Evergreen Academy. They guarantee admission to an elite college. I'll work on the finances." His pitch rose suddenly. "You do your part and I'll do mine, okay, baby?"

Veena's lower lip quivered and she let out a bawl. Raja gave the baby back to Usha. "She must need a change or something."

Usha stroked Veena's downy hair and thanked her a third time. She'd made Raja forget about the MBA. She held her close and knew she didn't want to further her education. Not now.

She only wished her mother could have been here.

As if on cue, the phone by her bed rang. "Congratulations, congratulations!" she heard her father's voice.

"How are you?" she asked.

"Fine. More importantly, how are you and how is the baby?

When Raja called with the news, he said she is beautiful and very intelligent!"

Usha laughed. "He would say that."

Her mother came on the line, weeping. "I should have been there. But what could I do? You have to manage all on your own. I feel awful."

"I can manage easily. Don't feel so bad. You couldn't come because of Appa's pneumonia. It's not your fault. He's okay now; that is important. We are fine, the baby and I. Don't worry. You know what? I'll come to India with the baby soon."

She knew that would give her mother something to look forward to.

After Veena came home, Raja continued his one-on-one bonding. He bought a rocking chair, and rocked the baby to sleep each night. As days went by, he didn't mention the MBA program. Usha relaxed.

Marcy visited often. She noticed the even rhythm of Raja's new chair. "I told you not to worry," she said. "I knew he would fall in love with her."

"You were right. But it's not right that you bring the baby so many gifts. You don't have to bring something every time you visit."

"Shopping for baby clothes is so much fun. They look adorable hanging on those racks. They're calling to me."

"Oh, you're silly. But seriously, please stop. It makes me feel guilty."

Marcy shushed her. "Stop talking. The baby's trying to sleep. Can't you see?"

In the family room, Raja intoned, "Academics are a must, of course. But you must focus on excellence in other areas, too; maybe an art form? And a sport? So what will it be? Swimming? We have good weather here for that. Or golf? Out state is famous for golf. There's time, of course. So, think about it."

Marcy raised her eyebrows. "What is he talking about?" she whispered.

Raja continued. "And we need something for that Indian element, *kutti*. Music, maybe? Maybe an instrument? You must build a great portfolio in the next eighteen years."

Usha dragged Marcy into the kitchen. "Ignore him. That's just his way of talking to her. He doesn't know any other way. Frankly, I'm glad he's not talking about my university classes anymore."

"Boy, he's sure setting some big goals for Veena. Transferring aspirations?"

"No. That's not it. He always aims for excellence and he expects the same of his family. That's just his way. And she's so little right now. Let him indulge."

"Are you going to stop your MBA program after spending a whole year on it?"

Usha pressed her lips together. There were some areas best friends should not step into.

June and July flew by in a flurry of bottles, diapers, and sleepless nights.

One night in the beginning of August, after Veena had fallen asleep, Usha collapsed into a chair at the kitchen table. Having been on her feet all day with a feverish infant, she needed to sit. Placing her legs on the chair across from her, she examined her swollen ankles and toes. A thought niggled. Perhaps it was time to get sandals a size larger—she'd read somewhere that a woman's shoe size increased after childbirth—she stuffed her feet into footwear too small.

Raja walked into the kitchen.

As if he'd forbidden her to sit, she jumped up, wiped her hands on a towel, and began organizing the sterilized baby bottles. "Do you hear the crickets chirping outside?" she asked, initiating conversation. "Aren't they loud? I heard they do that by rubbing their wings!"

She expected a response, not a question.

"How many classes did you sign up for this fall?" he asked.

Her feet throbbed.

Since Veena's birth, Usha hadn't said anything about her classes. He hadn't asked, and she hadn't discussed the program or the fact that she wouldn't be returning to the university. She hadn't registered for the fall semester.

"Umm… I picked some classes in February, a long time ago. I don't know, really." She lifted her toes off the floor, placed them back, then raised her heels. Pain shot through her calves.

"Well, go over tomorrow and check," he said.

Usha sat down at the table with some balm.

Will the smell bother the baby?

"What about Veena?" she asked Raja.

"What about her? Take her with you. You are only going to sign up for classes."

"And then what? I can't take her to classes with me."

"Well, what do other women do?"

Usha wanted to say, "*I don't care about others. I know what I want to do.*"

"I don't know," she said. "I haven't been in this country too long. I don't know what they do. But I know I can't leave a baby at home."

"Women go to work, don't they? There must be child-care facilities near the university."

Usha decided the pain balm had too strong a smell. She didn't use it.

"I cannot. I cannot leave this baby with a stranger. Come on."

"We've already invested two semesters into this program. Keep your goal in mind. Don't lose track."

Veena let out a yell for a diaper change and the conversation ended. Usha knew, though, that Raja wouldn't let it go. She'd fooled herself into thinking he'd forgotten about her classes. She'd planned a trip to India. Her parents wanted to see the baby.

Why do my feet, ankles, and calves hurt so much?

Desperate for a friend, Usha called Marcy. She reached her friend's answering machine. Something about talking into a machine made her hesitant, wary of leaving messages. The first time she dialed, she hung up. She tried again and left a semi-coherent message telling Marcy she missed her good cheer and optimism.

Marcy arrived without her trademark smile.

"Something wrong?" Usha asked. "Haven't seen you for over a week."

"Yes, everything's gone wrong." Marcy's habitual sunniness had deserted her. Her crumpled shirt looked as if she'd slept in it. "I've been so down. I haven't made meals for the past few days. I haven't picked up my mail from the box or even answered my telephone. I thought holding Veena would cheer me up. Where is she?"

"She's sleeping." Usha didn't recognize this Marcy. No make-up, clothes that could use a wash, messy hair. "Gosh, what happened? I thought you came because you got my message."

"What message? Did you call?" Marcy lifted dull eyes.

"Yes. I wanted to talk to you."

"Sorry. I've been miserable. My Montessori is closing because they don't have enough funding. So, I have to find another job."

"Oh, no. Are you okay? I'm so sorry. I've been so selfish."

"No, you aren't selfish at all. You let me see Veena whenever I want."

Usha tried to focus on the positive. "You'll find something soon. You have experience. Surely, you can manage in the meanwhile?"

"Larry is working part-time and he's still trying to finish his degree. I don't know what we'll do. Anyway, enough of my sob story.

What did you want to talk to me about?"

"It's nothing."

"Come on, tell me. I told you my story. You tell me yours. It's only fair."

"It's just that Raja brought up my classes again. He thinks I've already registered. But he doesn't understand my situation. He says I've already put in two semesters and he thinks I should finish."

Marcy cocked her head to one side and scratched her right ear. "He's right, you know."

Usha couldn't stop herself. "You're supposed to be my friend. Don't you understand? I can't leave my baby. And even if I did leave her at a daycare center, I don't think I can study, I'd be so worried. Besides, I was planning to take Veena to India and to stay there for a few months. Everyone wants to see her."

Marcy cocked her head to the other side and scratched her left ear.

"You're fussing for no reason. You could always go at the end of the semester, in December," Marcy said.

A bristle ran through Usha. Clearly, Marcy thought her own problems superior.

"But that's four months away."

"Well, it's easier with a seven-month-old than a three-month-old, don't you think?"

"But I'll get only four weeks at the most. Too short."

"Then, go in the summer. You'll have three months." Marcy expelled an exasperated breath. "Come on, these are just logistical issues. The bottom line is, you've invested so much into your education already. Don't quit now."

"But I still won't leave my baby with a total stranger, and definitely not in a daycare facility." Usha clenched her teeth.

Silence.

A wan smile broke through. It transformed Marcy's sad demeanor.

"You've got the solution in front of you."

"What?"

"Do you trust me?'

"Of course."

"Then, let me take care of Veena when you go to class."

For the first time since she met Raja, Usha understood the meaning of the word optimization.

11

Surprise Visit

July 23, 2012

*U*sha got to work early on Monday morning, woke up her hibernating computer, and printed out an agenda for the 10:00 A.M. staff meeting. While the agenda printed, she checked her email inbox. When she didn't see anything of importance, she told herself nothing earth-shattering could occur in the world of college admissions over a weekend. Unable to resist, however, she checked again seven minutes later. There were no new messages. She ignored the drench of disappointment and moved her curser to the *X* at the top right to close the window.

Arjay had said he'd email her about working with his school. He hadn't. She'd often heard people say, "We should get together sometime," an open-ended declaration, with no fulfillment scheme. Or, more often, "I'll call you." Mere sentences populated with words, they didn't indicate a wish or a desire. The enthusiasm with which people made such announcements did not translate to action, making them empty promises. Thoughts, words, and deeds ought to follow in that order. Arjay's exact words had been: "You don't mind meeting with me again, do you?" He'd added, more specifically, "I'll email you some thoughts. Please let me know what you think of them." She remembered his parting remarks, too. "Good-bye then. Would you think about what I said?"

She'd embedded his words in her brain. His email had yet to come.

She rose and picked up her papers for the meeting. Campus Station had five employees: three coordinators, one receptionist, and herself. Rosa, Heather, and Lisa, the three coordinators, waited in the meeting-cum-conference room in the back, going over their notes. Patricia, the bi-lingual receptionist-cum-office manager fielded an early phone call in Spanish.

Lisa and Heather discussed their upcoming presentations with school counselors in north Phoenix. They told Usha they'd be out for two days this week. Rosa, meanwhile, had back-to-back sessions every afternoon with college-bound students and their parents, helping sort out financial aid and scholarship issues before school started in the fall. Fluent in Spanish and English, she aided in translations as well.

"Usha, phone call on line one for you," Patricia interrupted.

"Just say I am in a meeting. Take a message, I'll call back," she said.

"Well, it sounded pretty important."

Usha jumped up. "I'll take it in my office."

"Excuse me," she threw over her shoulder. Three pairs of curious eyes followed her.

He'd called her. She was expecting an email. Before picking up the phone, she paused to still her smile.

"This is Usha," she said.

"Finally! Why don't you ever answer your cell phone? I called you at home, too…"

"Hello, Marcy. I wasn't expecting your call."

"Could you sound a little more excited and say, 'Nice to hear from you, Marcy?'"

"Sorry, it's Monday morning and I'm in a meeting. I'll call you this evening."

"Should I believe you?"

"I promise."

"Okay. I'll tell you in the evening."

"Tell me what?"

"Wait till the evening."

"No. Tell me now. Quick."

"Okay, I'm such a pushover. So, I'm coming to see you guys next weekend. I wanted to check with you before I buy my tickets."

"Lovely. Do come. Are you taking some time off from the business?"

"Usha! It's your birthday on Saturday. Don't tell me you forgot?"

"Yes," Usha laughed. "I did. In my calendar, next weekend's still far away. And yes, I'd love to have you visit. I've got to go now. I'll talk to you in the evening. I promise."

She had forgotten her birthday: July 28.

By the time she got back, the staff meeting had wound down.

"What did I miss?"

"Not much," Heather said. "I'll type up the minutes. Check your email in ten minutes."

When she checked her email, Usha saw Marcy had forwarded her airline itinerary. She would arrive late Friday evening. Heather had sent the minutes of their meeting. Nothing from Arjay. His words did not translate to action.

At 3:00 P.M., she noticed she was making mistakes in her calculations; she'd lost her concentration. "Time for some caffeine," she mumbled. She picked up her mug and made herself a cup of tea.

Outside, in the reception area, a boy lingered. No sign of Patricia.

"May I help you?" Usha noticed his neat appearance: hair combed, a plain white shirt with jeans, sneakers on his feet. Most teenagers who came in to their office looked as if they'd come straight from bed.

"Umm… I'm looking for some information." He held up a brochure.

"We're here to help if you're looking to get into college," she said.

"Umm… yes. I, I…" His fingers rolled and unrolled the brochure.

"Would you like to sign up for a workshop or are you looking for a one-on-one appointment with one of our coordinators?"

"I'm not sure. I…" He couldn't articulate what he wanted.

Where is Patricia?

Usha pointed to a sign-in sheet on Patricia's desk. "Write your name and contact information on this sheet and come into my office. I can help you." He wrote his name, Andres Garcia, on the sheet.

Standing outside her door, he shifted from foot to foot.

"I don't bite. Come in and take a seat." Usha smiled. "Tell me, are you a junior or a senior in high school and which school do you go to?"

"I go to Central School. It's pretty close from here. I'm a senior and I know I should, like, be applying for college admissions soon. But…"

Usha ignored his incomplete sentence. "Great! So you are thinking about college. That's good news. Do you know where you'd like to go?"

"I'm not sure. Like, there's this problem." He fidgeted in his seat, restless.

"Everyone has problems. The biggest one is the financial one. Are you afraid you can't pay for college?"

"Yes. And there's a bigger problem." He chewed on a fingernail. She noticed his bitten-down nails struggled to emerge from their nail-beds. "This is, like, confidential... My parents won't want me telling you this."

"Imagine I am a doctor. I can't help you unless you tell me your issue. Don't worry. I won't even discuss the issue with others unless I need help or a second opinion."

"Well, my parents are... my parents are what they call undocu-mented."

So that is his issue. His parents have no legal visa status in the US.

"They are laborers who work on farms. I was not born in the US, but I've been here since I was four."

Usha gulped. She knew she had to word her response carefully. "I see," she said. She understood his fears. He thought he couldn't attend college. "You know," she tried to encourage him. "You can still go to college. But you'd be treated the same as someone from outside the state. What that means is, your tuition would be consider-ably higher." She knew the government's financial aid programs and grants did not include students without legal status. State universities would not consider him eligible for in-state tuition at the moment. Soon, legislation might pass that charged students like Andres in-state tuition like other residents of the state. For now, however, the news remained dismal. She didn't want to discourage him. For all she knew regulations could change after his first year in college. "There are private scholarships you can apply for," she said. "How are your grades?"

"I'm in the top five percent of my class. I don't know if that is good enough."

"That's outstanding. Did you take your SAT, the Scholastic Aptitude Test, yet?"

"Yes, I've taken it. I got 2150 on my SAT."

"Fantastic!"

"Do you believe I can apply for scholarships?" In his eagerness, he moved forward in his chair. "I don't know how I can pay for college otherwise. My parents can't afford the fees, not even in-state tuition. I thought I could work and go to school and with some scholarship help maybe I could manage."

This is a tough one. It would be a shame if he can't go to college.

"Okay, here's what I can do for you. Before you go, let me give you a list of scholarships you'd be eligible for. Look them over. If you have questions, come back and see us."

He brightened and clasped his fingers together as if to stop chewing on his fingernails.

She produced a list from her drawer and marked the ones she thought he could apply for. "Here's the list. Do you know which schools you want to apply to?"

He shook his head. "Not sure. But I guess, like, you know, our in-state schools?"

"Okay, the application process is all on-line. We can help you with that when the time comes. We can also work with you on your scholarship applications."

He stood, his right hand clenched at his chest, arrested on its way to his mouth. "Umm... I want to say thank you." His eyes shone with imminent tears. "If I go to college, I'll be the first one in my family."

"You're welcome. That's what we're here for."

He left.

Usha's mug of tea had cooled.

I will do my best for Andres. Talented kids deserve an education.

She'd direct him to scholarships from outside sources. A few thousand dollars here and there would help some. What she hadn't told him—the scholarships wouldn't cover his entire tuition. Financially, only a complete tuition waiver from one of the universities could benefit Andres and his family.

She sipped her tea. It tasted curiously strong. Frowning, she examined her cup. The tea bag had split, spewing swirling tea leaves into her cup.

She thought about Andres. Life without a college degree for someone like him would mean being sentenced to lower-paying jobs with little prospect of upward mobility. There had to be a way.

She turned her monitor on and checked to see if she had any new messages.

There was one from Dr. A. Wheeler.

He can wait.

She threw out her tea bag, picked up her mug, rinsed it out, and grabbed a paper towel to wipe it clean. After placing the cup on a coaster, she went back to her email.

Arjay's note carried an oddly business-like tone. She clicked on the recipient list. It included two other people: Megan Bower and Andy Rodriguez. Arjay invited her to his campus on Friday, at 11:00 A.M. for a meeting with their Assistant Director of Outreach and Recruitment, Megan Bower, followed by lunch and a campus tour with Andy Rodriguez. He signed off with his name, below which his designation and contact numbers appeared.

He'd said he'd email her some thoughts. She didn't see any thoughts in the email. Instead he'd issued an invitation. She frowned.

When did I agree to visit his campus?

She read the email again and shook her head. One of the officials from Valley University could drop off any information they wished to share with prospective students. She hit the reply button. Fingers hovered over the keyboard. She'd tell him she had a previous appointment. Or she'd decline his invitation; no need for explanations.

She thought back to their last conversation.

"You don't mind meeting with me again, do you?" he'd asked.

And she'd answered, "Of course not."

She took her hands away from the keyboard, confused. Her palms pushed against her forehead. She attempted to organize thoughts. A reason for her to survey their campus didn't surface. Nor did a reason for her to meet other officials.

Isn't there a reason?

She had to go. One motive propelled her: Andres.

12

Field Trip

July 27, 2012

It took Usha half an hour to get to Valley University's visitor parking lot where she parked in the shade provided by a young palo verde tree. Mid-morning perspiration meandered down her spine. Strands of hair had escaped her bun and clung in wet swirls to the nape of her neck. The unrelenting sunshine made her squint behind her sunglasses.

Arjay had every reason to be proud of this campus. The grounds showed off young trees, lots of green, and pathways with an assortment of benches for students to sit and relax. Maps of the campus at strategic corners made it easy for visitors to find their way around. She noticed little activity on campus; few students enrolled in summer classes.

She knew she'd arrived early; she could not fight her habit. Arjay scheduled the meeting for 11:00 A.M. She didn't understand the urgency of her feet then as she scurried toward the Admissions Office, arriving breathless at the reception She asked the preoccupied student at the desk how she could get to Arjay Wheeler's office. He directed her to the third floor without taking his eyes off the computer screen.

She stood outside Arjay's closed door, wheezy as if she'd taken the stairs instead of the elevator, and rapped her knuckles on the door. When she heard no answer, she shifted her handbag from the right shoulder to the left and pursed her lips. He wasn't in his office.

This is inconsiderate, rude even.

Although this meeting might fall under the label of work, there were better things she could be doing with her time.

What now? How long should I wait?

This had to be the wrong room. She read the stainless steel name-plate outside his door one more time. *Arjay Wheeler, Director of Admissions.* She waited for two minutes.

She couldn't loiter outside his door. Frustrated, she turned her head this way and that, looking for someone who could help her. She didn't see anyone. There were only two options available: she could go back to the reception desk on the first floor or she could take a seat on the couch at the end of the silent hallway. She turned to walk in the direction of the couch.

She jumped as a voice rang out in the quiet corridor. "Usha!"

Hurried footsteps followed the voice.

"There you are. I was looking for you!" Arjay said.

"Of course I'm here. I thought we had a meeting scheduled." Her words—against her nature—sharp, acerbic even.

"I waited downstairs. We must have missed each other. Anyway, welcome to our campus. Sorry to startle you. I had a hunch you might be early."

Her mind absorbed: he'd waited downstairs. She asked, "What hunch?"

He didn't respond. Instead, he took her hand. "Thank you for coming!"

She wanted to hold on to her irritation, but it slipped away before she could embrace it.

Arjay wore a gray, collared t-shirt with a black pen clipped to his chest pocket. He'd paired the shirt with jeans and portrayed a casual, yet cool appearance. Raja wore formal attire to work, even in 110-degree weather. He liked the professional image.

Do I look wilted?

Her silk top clung to her back after walking across campus in the hot sun.

Keep your focus. This is for Andres.

He offered her a seat and a bottle of cold water, which she accepted.

She took the chair across from his and glanced around. Four hardcover books sat on the table, piled one on top of the other. Each one had scraps of paper sticking out from between pages—bookmarks to important passages. She would bet all the money in her handbag he'd marked those pages. She knew, once a compulsive highlighter, always one—the proclivity hard to break.

Can I tell him he is desecrating books?

His computer monitor boasted Post-it Notes stuck around its perimeter; he relied on physical reminders. He'd placed no knickknacks on the table; papers with scribbled notes in red along the margins littered the surface. She didn't see photographs of family, no mementos, nothing that told her anything about his personal life.

Still, he may be married or involved with someone.

"Thank you for coming to our campus. You'll be meeting the Assistant Director of Outreach and Recruitment soon. Her name is

Megan Bower. I was hoping you could meet the Academic Dean as well, but he had a family emergency today. Anyway, after lunch in our student union, Andy Rodriguez, the person in charge of campus tours, will take you around."

Usha remembered what he'd said in her office. "I'll email you some thoughts."

"I want to ask you something. I expected an email from you with some thoughts leading to a discussion. You didn't mention a visit when we last talked. Now, you fix up this meeting... and here I am meeting some other people? I don't visit campuses..."

Before he could answer, a rat-a-tat on the door preceded the entry of a petite, blond woman in her thirties.

Arjay rose to make the introductions. "Usha, this is Megan Bower. She's in charge of recruiting for Valley University. Megan, Usha."

"It's so nice to meet you, Usha!" Megan gripped Usha's hand. Her voice squeaked like that of a teenager. "Arjay told me about the great work you do at Campus Station," she continued.

Embarrassed warmth stole into Usha's chest.

"I am so looking forward to working with you," Megan went on. "As you can see, we are new and we are looking for good students. But we are also a great university with seven colleges offering over forty-five degree programs."

Focus on Andres and be upfront.

"Megan, at Campus Station, we do our best to get students into universities. But, let me be frank here. Those who come to us are from lower income groups. So, you see—"

Megan interrupted. "Yes, we can help. For us, it's the quality of the undergraduate that matters. We have financial aid packages that can make it possible for everyone to attend our university."

"You are a private college. Can you compete with the state schools in terms of tuition and fees? Can you offer good scholarships, in other words?"

Usha looked at Arjay. He remained silent, and his impassive expression gave nothing away.

"Everything can be worked out. Right now, our priority is to get the best scholars. We'll work on a case-by-case basis. When they graduate, they'll become our biggest ambassadors." Megan's words flew from her mouth in her high-pitched voice.

In Usha's mind, hope sprouted for Andres.

"So, what do you expect from us at Campus Station? I told Arjay, we'll be happy to display your brochures, your posters... anything. I can talk about your school when we talk about the other universities. What else?"

"Can Campus Station pick a date and send high school students over to us? One of you can accompany them."

"Sorry. Since I don't accompany students to the other universities, neither I nor anyone from Campus Station can accompany them to yours either."

"But you don't mind doing, like, a Campus Station field trip?"

Megan's usage of the word "like" reinforced Usha's initial impression.

"I wouldn't call it a Campus Station field trip. I am merely suggesting that you have an open house. I'd be happy to direct students to your event."

Megan's smile disappeared.

"Look," Usha said, "I cannot decide things unilaterally. I have to bring this up at our next staff meeting and see what we can do."

"That would be great. I'm thinking of a twice-a-year event, perhaps on a week day, when students can spend the day here."

"I can't ask students to miss a day of school."

Arjay broke in. "We do want them to check out a class or two here, meet some of our undergrads, and soak in the atmosphere. That won't be possible on a Saturday. How about this, we'll try to tailor this around spring break or fall break. Usually these breaks are different for high schools and colleges."

Megan brightened and smiled at Arjay as if he had presented her with a gift. Usha dug into her purse for her business cards—she remembered putting a few into her purse as she left her office. She offered one to Megan. "Okay, so send me an email with possible dates and we'll discuss this further."

"Thanks for coming. I'll keep in touch. Arjay told me Andy is going to show you around? I know you'll just love our campus."

"It is beautiful, yes. But I do believe the prettiness of a campus plays a small part when students decide whether or not to attend a university. Most of our students are driven by financial considerations." Usha knew she was deflating Megan's enthusiasm, but there were practicalities involved.

Ruffled, Megan rose from her chair. "Bye, Usha. It was so nice meeting you. Arjay, we'll see you tomorrow morning?"

Do they have a date? She is far too young, though. Besides, she's wearing a wedding ring. Arjay isn't.

He clapped his hands, breaking into her thoughts. "Are you ready for lunch? Andy, your tour guide, will be joining us. Unfortunately, Megan has another appointment."

Usha nodded and picked up her bag. "I'd like to talk to you about a student."

"We can talk and eat, can't we?" he said.

He took her elbow and ushered her out into the hallway. They walked to the elevator, which took a while to arrive. An inexplicable hesitation stirred at the prospect of being alone with him in an enclosed space. She almost suggested they take the stairs when the doors opened.

Talk. It won't seem quite so intimate, then.

"The campus is quiet."

"Quiet? Wait until school starts in a few weeks. It will be noisy then."

"How many are enrolled at this university?"

"Right now, about 9,000."

"Not too big."

"Most private schools are not large. Think how wonderful that is in terms of class size, the kind of attention given. Here, a student will never be in a class with 200 others, which often happens in large, public institutions."

The elevator dinged, indicating they'd arrived at the lobby. He reached for her elbow again, ushered her out of the elevator, and released his touch. She felt the imprint of his light fingers all the way to the student union and the Italian restaurant.

Raja did not believe in light touches.

As soon as they sat, Usha said, "I want to ask you this before my tour guide gets here. You didn't answer my earlier question. You said you'd be sharing thoughts via email, so why this visit to your campus?"

He patted her hand. "It's not that complicated. I moved to Phoenix from a university in Colorado only eighteen months ago. I'm proud of our campus and I wanted you to see it."

He took in her expression. "Not convinced?" he asked. "Do you want me to apologize? I'm sorry. Although I'm not sure what I'm apologetic about. I wanted you to check out our campus and meet some people. I believe experiencing something is better than just hearing about it."

Arjay did not point out she'd accepted his invitation.

She might complain, but she came here, an unnecessary voice reminded her. She shushed it. The fact remained: she hadn't declined his request.

Young Andres popped into her mind.

She said, "So, I'm sure you know there are good students who would love to attend college, but can't afford it."

"Yes, you mentioned them."

"There is one particularly complicated situation. The boy has great grades, but his parents are undocumented farm workers."

"Undocumented?"

"Well, they came to the US from Mexico, bringing the boy with them when he was young. And, somehow, they never got the legal paperwork done."

"That is a problem, at least for now. Just how badly does the boy want to go to a university? Is he committed to education?"

"It seems rather unfair to punish the boy for something he had no control over. He seems bright and has good SAT scores. It would be a shame if he couldn't go to school. He has funding issues in addition to the problem of his legal status."

"I can try and help. There's this consortium of Hispanic businesses that our college president is involved with. It offers full scholarships to five deserving students admitted to our university each year, based on both need and academics. A first-generation student, that is someone who comes from a family where no one has gone to college before, has a good chance of getting it. So I can—"

"Wonderful!"

"I said I can try, so let's not get too excited." He smiled. "Can you have the boy contact me?"

"I'll ask him to get in touch with you."

"Great! Wonder what's keeping Andy. Why don't we go ahead and order lunch? I'm sure he'll be here soon. They serve good vegetarian lasagna here. I recommend it," he said.

"I love lasagna," she said.

Raja loved lasagna, too.

Raja has come into my thoughts three times this morning. Why does he enter them now, when I am with Arjay? What will he say about this lunch? Why would he say anything about a business lunch?

"A business lunch?" Raja asked in her head. "If so, how did Arjay know so many things about you? Has he asked you about a husband?"

Usha clenched her fists together.

Why would he ask me about a husband, Raja? I'm not wearing a ring. You know I've never worn one.

Following custom, she removed her *thali*—the sacred symbol of marriage Raja had placed around her neck twenty-six years ago—after he passed.

"Then, answer this. How does he know that you are a vegetarian?" Raja asked. He'd always been thorough.

13

Birthday Hike

July 28, 2012

A t 5.30 A.M., Usha squinted against the rising sun to locate a parking spot. The lot, full of cars, bore evidence of hikers attempting to beat the heat.

"This Arizona sun is too much. It's unrelenting. How did I ever live here?" Marcy asked.

"The hike was your idea. In any case, the Waterfall Trail at White Tanks is so easy, seven and eight-year-old children can handle it."

"I wanted to for old times' sake. Nostalgia, maybe. Not at this hour, though. You're used to waking up early and you don't need sleep anyway. Not me. I don't think I've ever woken up this early on a Saturday."

"California, darling, you've forgotten. Look at the temperature,"

Usha pointed to the digital display in the car. "It's already 81 degrees."

With a deft swing she pulled into the last available spot. "Got water?"

Marcy heaved herself out of the car. "Got it."

"Let me check to make sure I have everything. Lately, I seem to forget things. Okay, so I have sunscreen, a couple of energy bars, cell phone, small towel, water. You all set?"

Marcy looked into her backpack and nodded.

The air retained warmth from the day before.

"This is just as I remember. Toasty," Marcy said. "Only, I was younger then," she made a rueful gesture.

"Take it easy. We can turn around whenever you want," Usha said. "I haven't done this for a while either."

The words, "Since Raja died," remained suspended in the air between them.

As if she understood, Marcy gave Usha an impulsive hug. "I know, birthday girl," she said.

Usha heard Marcy's labored inhalations and wondered if she could handle this easy hike, even for old times' sake. The monsoons may have departed but the humidity had not. Unusual for Arizona—the air, wet, heavy.

A path trodden flat by past hikers lay ahead. In five minutes, they stepped aside for two sweaty men jogging toward them.

"When do these people start to finish at 5:30?" Marcy said.

They found a pace and Marcy's breathing steadied.

"Two things," Marcy said, maneuvering her backpack into position. "I need to know two things immediately. Last night you escaped to bed. First, what's all this about a date? That's so exciting! And second, but no less important, what happened to that promised call last Monday? I never heard from you. Girl, are you trying to hide things from me?”

This Marcy, in more than appearance, had grown from twenty-five years ago. Then, she’d maintained a trim 120 pound figure and a polite formality. Today’s Marcy had an impressive girth and weighed in freely with her opinions; a confidence borne of her success in business.

Usha shook her head. “I sent you an email, didn’t I? I told you I’d be at the airport and I was.”

“Okay. I accept that. Are you trying to hide your dating?”

Usha mumbled. “Oh, it was nothing, just one meeting.”

“Hey, I know you mumble when you don’t want to tell me something. But this I need to know. It’s huge.”

“It’s not. Trust me, it’s not.”

“Well, I’ll be the judge of that. You are going to tell me everything.”

Marcy’s clothes matched her new persona. She wore the brilliance of an orange and pink shirt with the deep navy of a pair of Capri pants. After her divorce, she’d forsworn beige, gray, and olive.

A man following them alerted, “Right behind you.” They parted and allowed him to speed up.

Usha wiped her brow and adjusted her sunglasses.

Marcy gulped water, then asked, “Any plans?”

“For what?

“Your birthday, silly!”

“No. No plans. Besides, you are here. You are my plan.”

“What? No date?”

“No.”

“But I thought you said you were on a date last Saturday.”

Usha should have known Marcy wouldn’t let this go.

“It didn’t work out.”

"Why not?"

"Oh, just leave it. There's not much to say."

"I insist. Come on, don't clam up on me," Marcy said.

"I'm telling you, it was nothing."

"It's time you met someone. No need to feel embarrassed about a date."

"I'm not..."

"You're erecting barriers with me, my friend." Marcy stopped on the path. She cocked her head to one side and scratched her ear. "Let me tell you something from experience. You've closed the doors and windows for far too long. It's time to allow someone into your fortress. If you don't open the door, how will anyone enter?"

"First of all, it's not easy to get into a relationship with another man after being married for so long. I was used to Raja, not just the way he thought, but his body, his snoring, the way he ate, just every-thing about him. I'm also older now. I'm not sure I can adjust to being with another person. Stop being so dramatic."

In bewildered excitement, Usha had blurted out about the date to Marcy over the phone.

Perhaps the encounter with Arjay in the library caused a moment of mad-ness, made me abandon caution.

Meeting Joel in the library, in her mind, had now dissolved to a non-event. She didn't want to see him again. Neither did she want to discuss the date; the fear of revealing her vulnerability to her best friend plagued. She'd have to tell Marcy how she'd registered on a dating site and where the motivation came from.

And, I'll have to say how I foolishly assumed Arjay was my date from the website.

They came upon a couple taking photographs of a big boulder with clearly marked etchings.

"Petroglyphs," the man explained to the woman. "See these images carved onto the rock? These are called petroglyphs."

"Wonder how many hundreds of years ago these were made," the woman replied. "Do you know?"

Marcy chose to discontinue the conversation for the moment.

Usha thanked her stars.

Usha and Marcy passed them as the man said to his companion, "Some of these predate the Hohokam civilization."

"Makes you think, doesn't it?" Marcy said. "Many, many people have walked these very paths centuries before us."

"I know," Usha said. Lapsing into silence, they negotiated rocky terrain. Marcy didn't ask about Usha's date again. Occasional, indistinct voices carried in the desert and mingled with the twitter of birds and the buzz of bees. A twig snapped, startling them.

"What was that?" Marcy grabbed Usha's arm.

"Don't know. People have seen javelinas and coyotes here. And there are lots of little creatures, like rodents, around."

"Don't tell me!"

"Want to go back?"

"No. Just don't like the idea of a coyote alongside."

"I'm sure the animals know people hike these trails and stay away. Remember, we're in their territory, not the other way around. I hope there's water in the canyon at the end of this trail."

"It's called the Waterfall Trail, so there must be water."

"Only when it rains," Usha said.

"We go all this way and there's nothing to see, no water?"

"It's been raining off and on. We might get lucky."

Perspiration rinsed Usha's back. The two bottles in her backpack weighed like ten. Despite the gentle gradient, the heat made the walk arduous.

At the canyon, where the trail ended, several people stood, looking up at the thin trickle of a waterfall.

"Only in the desert," Marcy said, "only in the desert would a thin stream attract visitors!"

"Uh, huh…" Usha nodded, staring at a man in front of her. He wore a hat, his head tilted up. The khaki shorts and legs looked familiar, as did the height and the build. She shook herself. Men's legs had never been a preoccupation.

"It's so neat, isn't it?" a squeaky voice said.

She recognized the voice. Megan. With Arjay.

Am I so destined? Marcy. Now I have to make introductions.

Arjay patted Megan's back, the rumble of a laugh emanated. He turned to another man on his left.

"Let's go," Usha said, hurriedly.

"Why? We only just got here," Marcy said. "I need a break. Can we sit while I get a drink and a bite of my bar?"

Inevitable.

Arjay turned around as he heard their voices. Usha could not see his eyes behind the dark glasses, but his goatee moved as his mouth lifted in a smile.

"Oh, my God!" Megan squealed. "How nice to see you here. This is so cool, isn't it? Usha, meet my husband, Dennis."

Dennis stepped forward to shake her hand. Rugged and outdoorsy with tanned, muscular good looks and hair bleached by the sun, Usha decided he could be Crocodile Dundee's nephew.

"Dennis, this is Usha, we work with her. Well, sort of. Usha, do you like hiking? We've been showing Arjay the hiking trails around Phoenix, since he's new here. This week, we decided to drive west. And here you are!"

Megan liked to chatter.

I may not need to say much.

Arjay took her hand, and said, "Hello. Good morning!"

His composure annoyed her. "Good morning," she stammered.

In her head, thoughts rattled, popped, and burst like popcorn in a microwave. "This is my friend Marcy. She's from California."

"Nice to meet you. Here for a few days?" He remained polite, collected.

"Oh, no! I came for the weekend, to celebrate Usha's birthday." Marcy walked up to Arjay, shook his hand, and studied him.

Stop it, Marcy! Don't examine him. And you're dispensing too much information.

Usha swallowed, her throat dry.

"Birthday?" Megan piped in. "How nice of your friend to come and visit for your birthday."

Arjay lifted his sunglasses and looked at Usha, a question in his eyes. "Is it today?"

She wished he hadn't removed his glasses as if to take a closer look. Her face might show smudges of white sunscreen. She fought the urge to lick her parched, dry lips to moisten them.

Marcy answered for Usha, "Yes, it's today."

"Happy birthday," he said, and replaced his glasses.

Usha grabbed a bottle of water from her backpack and occupied herself with big gulps.

Marcy cornered Arjay and Megan. She pulled out a couple of business cards from the left pocket in her pants. Usha couldn't think of anyone else who would carry business cards on their person in a situation like this.

As she handed them around, she quizzed Megan and Dennis about their hiking adventures. She told them she had once hiked Camelback Mountain.

"Marcy, shall we head back?" Usha knew she spoke abruptly.

"Hang on," Megan said. "We're ready to get back, too. Let's all go."

Usha would have preferred to do without the camaraderie. Marcy's antennae would pick up nuances, her perceptions fine-tuned to decipher Usha's emotions and thoughts.

They turned around. In front, Marcy struck up a conversation about California real estate with Megan and Dennis, an agent. Arjay and Usha brought up the rear.

Silent, she prayed for her nerves to settle. Marcy had announced her birthday. At forty-nine, she didn't care about marking the day of her birth. The special event had become just that, another day.

"Did you get my email? You didn't respond."

Does Arjay want to goad me out of wordlessness?

"What email? When?"

"Yesterday."

"No. I didn't get an email from you."

"But I sent you one."

"And I'm telling you I didn't receive one." She knew she sounded curt.

Stopping to pull out her water bottle, she unscrewed the top and took a swig. The water didn't wash down her annoyance. *Is he going all official on me? Here?*

"Perhaps it went into your spam? Do you check your spam often?"

"I didn't get anything from you."

God! How long will we toss the conversational ball back and forth like this?

He held up a hand, as if to call a truce. "Would you bring... Well, I'm having an open house this evening. It's taken me a year and a half to fix up my house and finally, it's ready. I sent you the invite via email yesterday. Would you and Marcy come?"

She bit her lip to dam the words: *You're inviting us at this very last moment?*

"We have plans for tonight," she said.

He must feel obligated to invite us.

"Why doesn't he ask you if you have a significant other?" Raja asked. He'd made a habit of popping up with awkward questions.

She could not go to Arjay's house. As long as Raja kept inserting doubts into her mind, she could not. *Why? Will he think I am defying him? Or worse, cheating on him? I am not, for God's sake!*

She remembered Megan's conversation with him yesterday. At the time, she had wondered if Arjay and Megan had a date. Megan could have been referring to this hike or his open house.

"We can go either before or after dinner," Marcy piped up.

Sometimes Marcy's ears work too well.

A tiny creature scampered over Usha's foot and she took a dancing step backward, her foot landing on a rounded rock. As her knee buckled, Arjay's arm shot out to steady her, halting her collapse.

A frisson ribboned through her at his touch. She recaptured air and managed, "What was that?"

"Don't know. I didn't see it. Are you okay?"

She relieved herself from the unexpected embrace with a, "Yes, thank you," but the sensation of solidity and warmth stayed with her. She put some distance between their bodies.

Sensory matters should be irrelevant at my age. After all, my mother became a grandmother at forty-six.

Neither one of them brought up the topic of her near-fall again.

"Please come," he said before they split up at the end of the trail. "I'll resend the email as soon as I get home. The address and directions are included in the invitation."

She nodded.

His touch had confused her and rent her composure. She placed her fingers on her forehead and shut her eyes for a second as she tried to visualize her parking spot. *Where did I park? Marcy, stop asking questions.*

Marcy asked, "So, Arjay was *the* date?"

"What?" Usha asked, startled.

Marcy asked the question a second time.

"Whatever gave you the idea?" Usha's heart pounded like that of a teenager caught sneaking into the house past midnight. "We hardly spoke. Well, here's the car. Come on, get in." She'd never been happier to see her vehicle.

Marcy continued, "Sometimes what you don't say tells me more than what you do say. There's tension between the two of you. So much electricity, I thought I'd get burned if I got in the way." Marcy stood with the passenger door open, held her arm up, and then pretended to fall to the earth.

Usha cajoled a laugh. "And you got that from a conversation about emails? That's too funny. No, you're imagining it."

"Lie to yourself if you want. But he is as aware of you as you are of him."

"Our relationship is all business." That's what she'd tried to convince Raja when his voice echoed at lunch yesterday.

"Maybe you know him through your business," Marcy said, "but he wants more. The more important question is: what do *you* want?"

14

The Open Door

July 28, 2012

Usha knew. She knew as she subjected herself to a make-over with Marcy and Veena at Fashion Triangle Mall in Scottsdale. She knew as she tried to ignore the discomfort of the summer outfit—the sleeveless top revealed far more of her shoulders than she deemed appropriate—and as she teetered in matching red high-heels. She knew as Veena, Marcy, and she enjoyed massages on adjoining tables. She knew before Marcy brought up his name and reminded her of the invitation.

She would go to Arjay's house that evening.

Then why the pretense, the artificial protest, the elaborate ritual of reluctance?

She offered Marcy many reasons not to attend Arjay's open house. Theirs had been a long, tiring day. She didn't feel like getting dressed for a party after spending the day trying on dress after dress. They should spend one-on-one time. They got little occasion to share the minutiae of their lives. Veena would come home after her social engagement expecting time with Marcy; she'd promised to spend the night and have breakfast with them in the morning.

None of her reasons held water. They were too weak, only prevarication.

Arjay answered the door with a warm, "Hi!"

He followed that with, "Happy Birthday again, Usha." He then dazed her with the lightest of kisses destined for her cheek but mislaid at the corner of her mouth.

The gesture fed a shot of energy into her and erased tiredness in an instant. Such a feathery kiss, she might have imagined it. Then she saw Marcy cock her head to one side and realized the kiss had been real.

He ushered them into his compact living room with black leather couches and beige walls—clearly, a man's house. No fabric anywhere, not over the windows which featured plantation shutters, not on the cushion-less couches, or on the dining table. Cups, used paper plates, and rolled up paper napkins littered the coffee table and the end tables. Raja, restless, would have started clearing up with the guests still around. He did not like messes.

Am I making a mess of things right now? Accepting Arjay's invitation to this party? That accidental kiss?

"Thanks for coming."

When Arjay's trademark, uneven smile appeared, her heart did a somersault.

"Sorry we're so late," Usha said. "We've had a long, busy, day."

"I'm sure."

"Marcy insisted we should come." As if she hadn't wanted to. "She said it wasn't late. I don't like being late."

"It's definitely not."

Arjay introduced them to the four guests in his living room—parents of younger children in the middle of a heated discussion about violence shown in movies.

"Hey, everyone, meet Usha and Marcy."

"Are they your colleagues?" a lady asked Arjay.

"No. Marcy here's visiting from California. Usha and I," he hesitated, his eyes twinkling. "We met at a special place, the fifth floor of the Central Library."

Everyone laughed like he'd said something funny, but Usha's face burned as if he'd revealed an innermost secret. Marcy raised her eyebrows, cocked her head to one side, and scratched her left ear.

He pointed in the direction of the kitchen and offered drinks.

"Did Megan and Crocodile Dundee leave?" Usha clapped a hand over her mouth; she'd used her private name for Megan's husband. Her attention moved to Arjay's chest from where his laugh emanated.

"Nice moniker! Yes, they left."

"Water only for me, thanks," Usha said.

While he got Marcy her drink, Usha made her way to the living room with her bottle in hand, past the study on the left. The door to his study stood wide open. A woman's portrait in an eleven-by-fourteen-inch frame caught her attention. It hung over the computer desk, an accent lamp lighting the soft features of the lady in the picture.

Usha's feet hurt in the red high-heels. She found the nearest chair. Surreptitiously, she crossed her ankles and rubbed one painful foot against the other. Marcy's idea of style came with pain.

Usha didn't attempt to be social. The discussion on violent movies didn't grab her attention; instead, she found herself thinking about the woman in the photograph.

Marcy called from the doorway, sipping her wine. "Hey, Arjay is giving us a tour of the house. Come."

Fashion should not impose such punishment.

Usha grimaced as she stood and made a determination to jettison the high-heeled footwear the moment Marcy left.

She followed them to the patio outside, where a barbecue stood in one corner. "It'll be nicer to sit here once the weather cools," Arjay said. The four chairs in the patio still wore their plastic wraps.

A fountain gurgled in the center of the lawn. Marcy clapped her hands. "How wonderful, a running fountain. And with lights, too?"

"I just about managed to get it working yesterday," he said. "I'm finding out it's not easy to take an older home and fix it. There's still much to be done."

"You did all this yourself?" Usha pointed to the fountain.

"I find it cathartic. I've done a lot of things to this house, cosmetic stuff mostly. I removed all the old wallpaper, painted the house, and re-surfaced the kitchen cabinets. The back yard is a work in progress."

Usha remembered his hands; rough, as if he'd used more than just a computer as a tool.

He took them through his kitchen, where gleaming copper pots hung above the sink.

"Appliances, too?" Marcy asked. "Your refrigerator and dishwasher look spanking new!"

"The ones that came with the house were ancient. I had to get new ones," he said.

In the study, he'd placed only a desk, his computer, and the picture. Marcy wouldn't stay silent.

"That someone special?"

When Arjay did not answer, Usha looked at his face, devoid of expression. The movement of his Adam's apple, however, indicated emotion.

"My wife," he said in clipped tones "She died." As if he'd said too much, he asked, "Why don't we head upstairs?"

"I'm sorry," Usha whispered. If he heard her, his expression didn't reveal it. Instead, his arm guided her through the corridor to the two bedrooms above. In an unexpected flash of understanding, garrulous Marcy did not pursue the matter either.

"You've done a nice job on this house," Usha said. "I love this area. Central Phoenix is close to everything, the museums, down-town, and even the airport."

"That's why I chose it. I liked the location. But I also liked the idea that I could change the house to fit my needs."

Back in the living room, they found the heated discussion had simmered down somewhat—the guests picking up their plates and cups.

Usha located a seat. With her toes, she nudged the straps of her fancy footwear off and moved her feet under the chair furtively. She wiggled her toes. When she looked up, she found Arjay's eyes on her naked feet. Heat splashed her body.

Her callused heels needed attention; she eschewed footwear when-ever possible. Too late, she had an urge to hide her feet, but the strappy, high-heeled sandals didn't help. Along with the shopping and the massage, Usha wished Marcy had insisted on a pedicure.

Now he's seen my ugly feet.

Embarrassed, she rose and went to the kitchen for another bottle of water. She unscrewed the cap, took a swig, and looked out of the window at the fountain with winking lights.

Someone placed warm hands on her shoulders. She recognized the body without turning around.

Is it my imagination or is he drawing me to him?

She leaned back, closing the gap.

Images of a bubbling pot on the stove and the warmth of a man's loving touch surfaced in her consciousness. She'd leaned back against her husband on a magical evening in the past, when they'd been enticed by a sunset that featured dancing fountains and the titillation of ice cream.

Her heart bouncing as if she'd sullied the memory of that day, she jerked aside in an attempt to put some distance between Arjay and herself. Water from her open bottle splashed on the floor.

She placed the open bottle on the countertop; it rocked back and forth as if echoing the movement of her heart. Grabbing a few paper towels from the holder nearby, she said, "I am so sorry, so sorry."

"Relax. It's just water. Here, let me." He took the towels from her, mopped up the spill, and threw them into a bin. "I came to tell you I have something for you. So, hold on. Don't run."

By the time he returned, she'd regained her composure. He handed her a wicker basket filled with tomatoes, peppers, and eggplants.

"Happy Birthday!" he said. "I hope you enjoy these. They're from my garden."

She stared at the basket. Unlike the tomatoes in a grocery store, even-shaped and shiny-red, some of Arjay's tomatoes grew large, others small. The basket contained round ones and oval ones and a few misshapen tomatoes with deep lines running outward from the center. The eggplants, too, smaller than the ones in the store, didn't show off a deep purple.

"The peppers can be hot. You have to taste them to know. Luck of the draw."

"Thank you." *Now he is giving me gifts? Is this proper? I should say something.* "I love to cook."

"That's good. But I'd like to take you to dinner tomorrow."

"Dinner tomorrow?"

Why am I repeating his words?

"Open the door," Marcy had said.

"It's not that easy," she'd answered.

And he is so sure I don't have a husband?

"Yes, I'm inviting you to dinner. Marcy is leaving tomorrow, right? So you're free after she leaves."

"I don't know…"

Puzzlement swept across his face. "I don't understand," he said. "We've already had coffee together, lunch together. Why is this any different?"

Marcy popped her head into the kitchen.

How much did she hear?

"I'll send you an email with details. But in the meantime," he said, "can you send me your cell number?"

A question darted into her mind. *What will excellent Raja say?*

"Open the door, let someone in," Marcy had advised. Usha had opened the door on that day in the library, the day she met Arjay. The path preordained, inexorable.

15

Betrayal

July 29, 2012

Sunday morning, Usha jumped out of bed. Joyful energy bathed her body; a sensation she hadn't been acquainted with in the recent past. The intentional calm she had cultivated in the past couple of years disappeared. She changed out of her caftan into a flowery skirt and adjusted the waist in front of the mirror. When she combed the knots out of her hair, she didn't wince or groan. Since Raja's death, she'd lived in a detached manner, alive but not full of life.

She looked at her reflection and decided her arms looked more graceful this morning, longer and leaner.

The massage yesterday is the reason for this.

Working with clever fingers, the masseuse had eased clusters of muscle tension. Moving closer to the mirror, she noticed how her skin shone after the facial. She smiled as she recalled the shopping trip and the clothes Marcy had purchased. The two people she cared for most in the world, Veena and Marcy, were under her roof—reason enough to be happy.

She planned her breakfast menu while she brushed her teeth.

Can I make steel-cut Irish oats, sprinkled with cinnamon and brown sugar and topped with sweet papaya? Or will a broccoli, spinach, and mushroom frittata be more interesting? I'll make yogurt parfaits. I have blueberries, strawberries, and homemade granola, which I can layer with the yogurt. And of course sweet, milky, Indian tea spiced with ginger.

Raja preferred coffee. When he did drink tea, he used a tea bag and hot water. He said he found Indian tea too sweet, too strong. She had adapted to his tastes; making the spiced tea for one person became too much effort.

This morning, she craved Indian tea.

First, she set the Irish oatmeal to cook and diced a ripe papaya. She pulled out three short, wide glasses to assemble the parfaits and placed them on the table next to Arjay's gift basket of homegrown vegetables.

The vegetables should go into the refrigerator; the hot weather can ruin them. Despite the woefully misshapen tomatoes and the eggplants stunted and pale, she knew the homegrown vegetables would be delicious. She decided to make eggplant parmesan and use the tomatoes in a spaghetti sauce.

She'd promised Arjay she'd email him her cell phone number. Powering on her laptop, she sent him a one-line note.

She set breakfast on the table at 7:30 A.M. No sign of movement from Marcy or Veena. After pouring herself a cup of tea, she turned the television on, and flipped through channels to find *Meet the Press*. Since Tim Russert died, she hadn't watched the show. Raja watched it every Sunday. It occurred to her she didn't know if Arjay watched any of the Sunday morning programs.

She stretched her legs out on the coffee table and pointed and flexed her stiff toes.

Perhaps I shouldn't have imprisoned them in the red footwear yesterday.

She lifted her feet off the table; the tiled floor felt cool. She recalled Arjay's amusement at her clandestine efforts to ease the discomfort in her feet last night.

He surprised her with his many facets. He worked in higher education, and the work he had done on his house proved he could be good with his hands, too. She liked his home, the touches he'd added. Clean lines, no fluff. Like him. He'd been direct, asking her over to his open house yesterday, inviting her to dinner tonight.

What can I wear? Certainly not the uncomfortable red things on my feet. The restaurant he chooses may warrant formal wear, or perhaps I can get away with semi-formal clothing?

And I must tell Veena. Will she be happy for me?

She took a sip from her cup. A spice-laden aroma drifted to her nose, before the delicious warmth slid down her throat. Tea like this, shared with family, became satisfying, nostalgic even. She had an urge to awaken Veena.

She walked up to her daughter's room and knocked. Veena slept on her side, facing the wall. When Usha touched her shoulder, she startled awake, and groaned, "Whaaat?" like a teenager.

"Breakfast is ready. It's time to wake up."

Veena nodded, and said, "Five minutes." She turned to face the wall again, pulling the sheet over her shoulder.

Usha sat on the bed and looked around the room. She'd asked Veena to take some of her things when she moved out to her own apartment a while ago, but this room still remained a timeline to her daughter's life. One wall boasted pictures of dance events she had participated in through her childhood and college years. Parallel shelves on another wall displayed her many academic trophies.

Someday soon, I will pack everything and send it to her place. They'll make valuable souvenirs for her children.

Through the open door to the closet, Usha saw Veena's jewel colored prom dresses. She recalled Raja's reluctance; he hadn't wanted Veena to waste time attending Junior or Senior Prom, the end-of-school ritual every high school student looked forward to. Veena could probably still fit into those gowns.

Noises from the kitchen caught her ears. Marcy had awakened.

"Good morning. Thank God we didn't schedule another hike this morning," Marcy said when she saw Usha. "I needed my sleep."

"Are you ready for some tea?"

"Oooh, yes."

She took a sip and closed her eyes. "Wonderful. You make the best tea."

"I gave you the recipe years ago. All you have to do is follow it."

"You know I'm a terrible cook. It doesn't taste the same when I make it."

"Thank you. Take a flight from Los Angeles anytime you need some tea."

Marcy's phone rang.

Usha raised her eyebrows. "David?"

Marcy nodded. "Excuse me."

Usha had heard about David: the latest in Marcy's list of male friends. She believed this could be serious since he'd been around the longest, about three years. After her divorce, Marcy had told Usha she'd renounced marriage or even a long-term relationship. Until now. Her closeness with David could also explain why Marcy encouraged Usha to open the door and let someone in.

"Oh man, so much action early in the morning. Why can't you guys keep it down," grumbled Veena as she walked into the kitchen, tablet and cell phone in her hands. She took a seat, placing the computer and phone onto the kitchen table. Crossing her arms on the table, she settled her head on her arms.

Usha warmed a cup of tea and placed it by Veena. She waited for the aroma from the spices to tickle Veena's nose. She watched as her daughter raised her head, took a sip from the cup. "Yum," she said. "Thank you!"

"Awake?" Usha asked.

"Yup! Where's Masyma?"

As a child, Veena had bestowed a creative name upon Marcy. No one corrected her.

"Who wants Masyma?" Marcy said, as she came into the kitchen, giving Veena an expansive hug.

Usha felt an odd discomfort in the region of her heart. Years ago, she'd resented the bond between her friend and her daughter. The child had been entirely too happy going to Marcy's after school. Marcy was able to take a look at Veena's grades first. She'd check her homework, and sometimes read notes from teachers before Usha could.

"How's David?" Veena's expressive eyes danced.

"Oh, he's just jealous I'm having the time of my life with the two of you." Marcy settled herself on a chair and picked up her half-empty cup of tea.

"So, when do we get to see him?"

"You'll see him when you come to California. But tell me about you. Are you seeing anyone?"

"No time. Life is all about work right now. Work and more work." Veena made a moue of discontent.

"This is ridiculous. Here I am, an old lady, talking about my boyfriend. You should be the one talking about a special someone."

"Work consumes me right now. In a couple of years, I'll be ready.

Mother is the one you should focus on. She should find someone. She worries me."

"Hello! I happen to be in this room," Usha said. "And can we get to breakfast, please? Why is that device here?" She pointed to the tablet.

"I'm expecting some messages."

Usha shook her head.

The oatmeal turned out perfect, smooth and creamy. As she finished, Veena licked the remnants off her spoon. "So, Masyma, when are you getting married?"

"I don't know."

"You should get married. Then perhaps Mother will get inspired and get married, too."

Marcy cocked her head to one side and scratched her ear. "You want your mom to meet someone?"

Usha picked up the empty cereal bowls and placed them in the sink. "Excuse me, I am here, you know?"

Marcy continued as if Usha hadn't spoken. "I've been saying the same thing. In fact, Veena, your mom…"

"Anyone for more tea?" Usha interrupted, hoping Marcy wouldn't blab about her date with Arjay tonight.

Veena peered into her computer. For once, Usha did not object.

"So," Veena, said, "did my mom tell you I registered her on a dating website? Mother, did you even check it out? I reminded you more than once to get on it."

"Wow! That's exciting!" Marcy clapped her hands on the table.

"I don't think I want to."

"Why not, Mother? You don't even know who responded. I already paid the membership. Come on, take a look."

"I can't log in. No password."

"I knew you'd say that. I've written myself a note. Hold on."

Usha could not escape now.

Marcy winked at Usha.

Veena fished out a piece of paper from her purse. "Okay, Mother. Don't lose this again. Check it out. Here, sit." She turned the tablet in Usha's direction.

Usha typed in the user ID and password. A grin forced its way out. Ten men were interested in her.

Really?

She clicked on the first profile from the recommended list. Her smile vanished.

Everything froze: time, her fingers on the computer, and her thoughts.

The ebullience she'd woken up with disappeared.

It couldn't be. Yet, there it was: the familiar face with the neat goatee. Even if she could convince herself the photograph only resembled him, the name and the personal details—everything reinforced what she already knew.

"You have messages," blinked in green on the screen. She didn't yield to the invitation.

He knows all about me from the profile details, the photograph Veena has uploaded. When?

She logged out and closed the browser.

"What's wrong?" Marcy said. "You look pale."

"Nothing. I'm fine." She pulled her lips apart in the semblance of a smile.

"What about *Love After Loss?*" Veena expelled a forceful sigh.

"I'll look at it later, when I have more time."

Veena and Marcy exchanged glances. Her daughter shrugged.

As the freezing sensation melted, Usha's distress fueled an unexpected burst of energy.

I've been such a fool. I'm a terrible judge of character.

She pushed aside thoughts that wanted to hurtle through her psyche. She emptied the remaining oatmeal into a plastic container.

I need to load the dishwasher.

Arjay's methodology had been smooth. Behind that educated, polished, solicitous exterior, lurked a cheat, an internet predator. Not a clue had escaped. Of course, he had the benefit of experience and foreknowledge. She should be livid, instead all she felt was betrayal. A few moments ago, she'd been chilled, now perspiration sopped her sleeves.

From afar, she heard Marcy say, "Usha, let me help. Please."

A ringing.

Who is calling me at home on a Sunday morning?

No matter. It gave her a task. She needed to answer.

The man introduced himself as Security from the library. "A glass window has shattered. We are not sure if someone tried to get into your office."

The front window at Campus Station had a crack running through it, a fault line. She'd noticed it over a year ago. The fracture grew, like the roots of a tree, shooting out thin, secondary lines on either side of the main break. Unable to bear the strain any more, the glass crumbled.

Security doesn't know that.

"I don't think so. We have nothing of great value in there."

"Could you come by and check to make sure?"

This could be God-sent.

"Yes. I'll be there in a bit."

Veena and Marcy waited with expectant looks.

"That was Security from the library," Usha told them. "One of the windows in our office broke and they think someone might have tried to break in. I have to go to the office."

Veena did not hide her dismay. "I was hoping to take you both to my apartment. I thought I'd order lunch."

A reprieve. Perfect.

"I can't go. But take Marcy. She'd love to see your place; you've done such a nice job with it."

Busyness allowed her to erect a damn against cascading thoughts. She poured the remaining tea down the drain and loaded the dishwasher.

Memories of incidents she'd dismissed as coincidence insisted on surfacing in little bits and pieces.

Raja had prodded her with questions on several occasions, asking her how Arjay could have known she was a vegetarian. Arjay had never asked about her husband. He knew she was a widow. He knew she worked in education.

And he hadn't said a word.

Why? Is he stalking me?

She decided she'd never go up to the fifth floor of the library again.

He knows where I work. He knows everything. Perhaps Raja is right. I'm not smart enough to ferret out the truth. And I have no experience dating, none at all.

She'd never felt so vulnerable, or so stripped, in her life. Arjay intruded into more than her physical world; he made inroads into the inner workings of her mind, into areas she guarded closely. He even knew her birthday. Feverishly, she changed clothes. She couldn't wait to leave the house and the ugliness of her discovery behind. The man from Security waited for her at the library.

She should go and check on the broken glass.

⌒⌒

When she returned, she didn't find Veena and Marcy at home.

Usha lay on her bed, staring at a framed picture of Raja and herself on the nightstand. Prodded by young Veena, Raja had made reservations at a roof-top, revolving restaurant—Café 360 Degrees—for her 40th birthday. For the first time, they had dined out without their daughter, just the two of them. Conversation meandered around Veena, his work schedule, bills, and choosing from the menu items—married people conversation. And then, Raja surprised her with a gift of earrings, delicate diamond drops. She knew he couldn't have done it on his own, Veena helped him. Still, her mouth dropped open at her husband's unexpected gesture. Their exuberant waiter had captured the moment in the photo, asking undemonstrative Raja to place his arm around her waist and touch his cheek to hers.

"Give me a sign, Raja," she said to the photograph. "I don't know what to do."

He didn't respond.

Veena and Marcy took their time.

Maybe they are shopping for more clothes. Marcy likes buying colorful shirts.

Her phone dinged with a text message. "About time, Veena," she said.

Her phone displayed a brief message from Arjay. "6:00 P.M. at Café 360 Degrees. Look forward to seeing you."

He'd picked the most romantic restaurant in town.

Or perhaps Raja has sent me a message.

She couldn't overlay this date on the memory of that long-ago birthday dinner with Raja.

One of her associates at work could handle the official side of things with Valley University.

She wouldn't show up for dinner.

She made a fist, hitting her pillow hard, over and over again.

Damn him. Damn him. Damn him.

16

Rising above the Ordinary

November 1988

*U*sha believed Raja's obsession with charting out Veena's life path took root on the day they hosted their first party. Eighteen months had passed since the baby's birth.

She woke up at four that morning to start preparations. Apart from the cooking, she had many tasks to complete: clean the house, arrange the flowers on the dining table, chill the drinks, and set the plates and the silverware out. By the time the toddler woke up at seven, Usha had a head start, having completed half the cooking.

She heard Veena's, *"I'm awake, come get me,"* cry and rushed to pick her up from the crib. The toddler's diaper felt heavy and sodden. "Raja," she called. "Where are you?"

When she didn't hear a response, she remembered. He'd called out as he went into the study, "I have a telephone meeting for an hour." Work would not disappear because they had a party that night. Again, apprehension fluttered in the pit of her stomach. She tried to shake off nervousness and told herself she could handle the party—the food, the drinks, the number of people.

She'd attended two official gatherings: a Christmas party at the office and a retirement event at a restaurant. On both occasions, her average self surfaced, making her feel inadequate, gauche, and over-whelmed. The other spouses oozed confidence: they matched wits with each other, professionals tossing and parrying words, discussing work, trends, fashion, and news. Tonight, she had to hide her deficiencies, don graciousness, exude warmth, and hospitality.

Marcy called mid-morning. "Thank God," Usha muttered. By the time Usha wiped her hands on the kitchen towel and got to the phone, Raja had already picked it up. As always, he kept it brief.

"Thanks, for offering to babysit. But I think we'll be okay, Marcy." He hung up.

"Why didn't you give me the phone?" Usha asked. "It might be easier if Marcy took care of Veena this evening. Why did you turn down her offer?"

"Is there a problem with wanting my colleagues to meet our daughter?"

A sharp pain shot through her mouth as she bit the edge of her tongue. She wanted to ask him, *"How am I expected to host a dinner party and take care of this child at the same time?"* She didn't have the time to delve into such issues.

She put Veena down for a nap in the afternoon. Already, her child exhibited traits of the terrible twos, sometimes throwing tantrums that left Usha helpless. While the baby slept, Usha completed the cooking. After Veena woke, Usha fed, bathed, and dressed her. She handed Raja the child and told him she needed the next two hours for the finishing touches. He smiled at the happy child.

Fourteen and a half hours since she rose that morning, she dressed in a new sari. As she stood in front of the full-length mirror, she decided the soft sari draping gently over her left shoulder gave her a graceful air. The dress and the skirt she'd tried on before the sari went back into the closet; they'd lost the competition.

She checked on the food in the oven.

Perfect.

She understood the trick lay in making it all seem effortless, efficient. When the doorbell rang at seven, she squared her shoulders, ready to face her first guests.

Richard and his wife stood at the door. The glamorous Cindy shimmered in her black sheath of a dress and long silver earrings, blue eye shadow and big, blonde hair completing the look. The inadequacy Usha'd tried hard to suppress surged again; she hated her braided hairstyle, wished she'd done something else with her tresses.

"Hi! Nice to see you again!" Cindy exclaimed. She gave Raja a hug as she handed him a bottle of wine.

Cindy's effusive greeting and Raja's obvious look of admiration took Usha aback. Of course, he would respect her. The glamorous lady held a high-powered job as consultant with McKay and Company. With little time to dwell on his esteem, Usha filed the thought away for later consideration.

She'd made three kinds of appetizers which she placed on the coffee table while Raja got the drinks. Cindy took Veena from Raja and sat with the baby on her lap.

"Oh, what lovely hors d'oeuvres," Cindy said. Usha had never heard the words before. She only knew they sounded vaguely

French. Another question filed away for later.

"Thank you," she said.

Cindy didn't hear her. She was busy with baby Veena, "A is for…? B is for…?"

Usha grinned to herself, shaking her head. Cindy didn't know the first thing about babies.

How can an eighteen-month-old know the answers to Cindy's questions?

The baby responded to every question with a beatific smile.

What Cindy said next wiped out Usha's private thoughts.

"Raja, you haven't started your daughter on the alphabet yet? By now, our Amy knew her alphabet. She could recognize the letters from a chart and numbers, too."

Unused to being less than the best at anything, he stammered, "Isn't she a little young?" He moved forward to sit on the edge of his chair.

"Oh no, not at all. To get ahead, one needs an early start. Our Amy was reading by three. She finished high school at the top of her class, was a National Merit Scholar, an Intel Science Talent Search semi-finalist when she graduated high school, and now she is at Harvard. If you don't start now, how is your baby ever going to get into an Ivy League school?"

A bitter taste stole into Usha's tongue. She disliked the unknown Amy for her perfection.

What about allowing my baby to remain a baby for a while longer? And who's thinking about Harvard anyway? For heaven's sake, she's not even toilet trained yet. This is preposterous.

She wished Raja would come up with a strong defense.

Instead, she saw Raja's eyes light up. She recognized the precise moment when a spark touched them. She retrieved an empty plate from the coffee table and returned to the kitchen as if to get a refill. Anything to move away from Cindy, the person responsible for kindling that maniacal flame in Raja's eyes.

Usha had never hated anyone in her young life—until now. Her emotions tended to stay passive, punctuated by odd bursts of annoyance and occasional sadness. Hate manifested as a new emotion, albeit a strangely energizing one. She sped under its influence as she warmed up dinner, her movements imbued with renewed efficiency. Her face and body felt warm. Her head pounded. She knew she shouldn't allow a casual acquaintance like Cindy to have so much power over her feelings. Yet, she hated Cindy and hated hating her.

She gave the negative emotion full access to her psyche for the most important reason in the world: her child.

The doorbell rang again and again after that. Usha had to roll thoughts away. She'd unfurl them later, after the party. The baby, bless her, continued to behave herself. Usha received many compliments on the dinner and everything went off without a hitch.

The next morning, Raja went to a teaching supply store, bought two large posters, one displaying letters and another exhibiting numbers.

"What are you doing?" Usha asked. "She's too young for this, *illeya?*"

"*Illai*," he said. "They're never too young to learn."

"Come on, Raja, she can barely say Amma and Appa."

"See, the problem with you is you are so negative about everything. You never think of what is possible, instead you harp on what you think is not possible. If we want excellence, we must pursue it."

"No...," she began.

"Don't say 'no.' We must rise above the ordinary."

Hurt that he called her ordinary when she believed she'd thrown a marvelous dinner party only the day before, she turned away from the room. She needed to be alone for a while.

He'd found a new project at home: his child. He installed a chalk board in the baby's room and got himself a pointing stick. He handled Veena with infinite patience, as he pointed to the letters on the poster. Her attention wandered often; she was a toddler after all. Still, he plodded on as he executed what he called his grand plan. His immediate plan: for Veena to read and write by the time she started Kindergarten. And then, he'd find the best private school for a strong educational foundation.

"You do your part, and I'll do mine, okay?"

Veena ignored him and transferred her attention to the blocks near her. When she became bored with them, she reached for her favorite legless doll.

Usha cursed the day Cindy set foot in their house. She wished they'd never met. She parceled her arguments neatly, imagined writing them down and mailing them in a letter. What worked for Cindy's Amy may not work for her Veena. Every child grew at her own pace. Eventually, the learning curve leveled out.

It gave Usha great satisfaction to direct her anger Cindy's way.

Cindy didn't respond. Usha didn't mail the letter.

Raja said something to Veena. He repeated the statement.

Why is he repeating the sentence?

Usha listened.

"You must build a great portfolio in the next sixteen years," he said to the baby.

His statement rang familiar. Not because he'd just repeated the statement twice in a row.

Didn't he say it in the past?

Usha knew she'd heard him say it. She slapped her forehead.

Of course. Right after Veena's birth.

She shouldn't blame Cindy. She'd been wrong. Wrong in harboring all that fury, all those hate-filled thoughts, and wishing her the worst.

Raja had had ambitions for his daughter simmering inside of him before; before her birth. Ready to absorb Cindy's suggestions, he had soaked them up like pancake would syrup.

After all, Raja—an immigrant with dreams—pursued only excellence.

17

Juggling Acts

1993 – 2005

Raja left Veena with a lasting legacy: the skill of multitasking. She learned the art early in her life.

On the first day of school in the fall of 1993, Raja and Usha accompanied Veena to the second grade classroom. After she set her things down, Veena didn't greet the teacher. She glanced around the classroom and burst into tears.

"It's okay, *chinna kutti*," Raja tried to encourage her. "You'll do very well in the second grade."

"Where are my friends?" she cried, wiping off tears with the back of her hand. "I want my friends!"

"Don't worry, you'll make new friends here," Usha hugged her tight to reassure her.

"I want Sally, and Christina, and Derek. Where are they?"

"They are in another classroom, darling."

"But I want to be with them. I don't like this classroom. Every-one here is so big. I'm scared."

Raja tried reasoning with her and found adult logic didn't work with children. Veena wailed. She wouldn't stop. Until she did, they couldn't leave. The bell rang, and the teacher cleared her throat in readiness for the pledge of allegiance they recited each day. Usha apologized for the disruption and urged Raja and Veena to leave with her.

They walked into the principal's office. Even as Usha presented her request to move Veena back into the first grade classroom, Raja insisted he didn't want his daughter to take a step back. He wanted her to skip the first grade. Eventually, they achieved a compromise. Veena would take Math with the second grade class.

Veena juggled and enjoyed being with her first grade classmates while attending math classes with the second graders. Thus, she took the first step toward multitasking.

Inspiration next hit Raja when the family attended an Indian classical dance recital. He knew nothing about *Bharathanatyam,* but the three-hour solo performance impressed him. "Let's talk to the teacher after the performance," he said.

"For what?"

"So we can get Veena started on dance."

Usha pressed her lips together. This idea came with two sides, good and bad. Good: Veena would learn about their heritage; bad: it might become too much for the child. So far, Raja had focused on academics. If Raja expected Veena to put in the same sort of energy into dance, the stick-thin child could become overwhelmed.

"What about Veena?" she whispered. "Don't you want to ask her?"

"Since when does a six-year-old get consulted?"

He shared his dreams with Usha. When Veena got into high school, she'd be ready for her solo dance debut. He believed she should use the performance to further a worthy cause. "What a wonderful way to embellish her resume. It's all about setting goals," he told his wife.

Veena started Sunday morning dance classes. Either Usha or Raja drove Veena forty minutes each way to the dance class, making their weekends that much shorter. Usha tried to get grocery shopping, laundry, and cooking done in bits and pieces, overwhelmed with tasks that she could never complete. A half-finished curry remained on the stove, a load of laundry waited in the basket, and forgotten, overflowing garbage cans sat in the garage.

On weekdays, she went from chore to chore, flurried with office work, meetings, and deadlines. Her boss annoyed her. He imposed deadlines without comprehending her pressures, her lack of time, or her family obligations.

The whirl of intense activity didn't bother Raja. He pushed. Time constraints notwithstanding, he enrolled Veena in an after-school reading and mathematics program. She went to the learning center twice a week. He didn't account for intangibles: a child's feelings, the family's quality time at dinner, and simple outings like a trip to the local zoo.

Usha worried often.

How can all of this be possible? How can a person excel at everything?

She protested to Raja, "When is it going to be enough? You have a worthy goal, doing well in school. That is good enough for me. When does she get to be a child and just play with friends or watch television?"

She knew his answer even before he enunciated the words. "One needs to be well-rounded to get into a good university. You know that."

By the time she graduated elementary school, Veena had won every conceivable academic award the school could bestow. Raja kept his eye on the big picture, building a portfolio, so Veena could get into an elite, private high school.

Veena needed to show substantial results by representing the school in competitions. When she won the district spelling bee, Raja became dizzy with happiness. When the teachers chose Veena to represent their school at the state mathematics championship, he became delirious. He visualized Harvard mailing them an acceptance package.

Veena received many awards. However, she didn't get as much as a mention in the athletic area. She didn't play a sport.

Until tennis entered her life.

Raja took charge again. Veena played tennis Monday and Thursday evenings at the local recreation center. His work hours meant he couldn't watch her play often. But when he did, he became completely invested in the game. The normally controlled, polished man became crazed, shouting and screaming from the sidelines. "Get to the net, volley, volley." Or he'd yell, "That should have been an easy overhead!"

At one match, he became apoplectic when she failed to anticipate her opponent's backhand placement. "She's so predictable, so predictable… Get to the baseline," he said.

Usha saw Veena's lips quiver. "Raja, you're rattling her. Let her play," she said.

His face turned a mutinous red, chest heaving with repressed anger.

"Come on, I'm only being constructive," he told her. "I want her to have a fire in the belly. Why doesn't she have it?"

A match official approached Raja, asked him to move back, and keep it down. He stood by him until the players completed the match.

Raja accepted the official's censure. It took him longer to accept Veena's quality of tennis. For a while, he'd wake her up at 5:30 A.M. and hit a few balls with her before she went to school. He stopped setting the alarm when Veena decided she didn't want to play tennis any more.

However, as a natural dancer, Veena took pride in her technical expertise and her creativity. She spent endless hours learning about the accompanying music and choreography.

At fourteen, she added an extra class each week, in preparation for her solo-dance debut, the *arangetram*.

She began ninth grade at the best private school in the Phoenix area: Evergreen Academy. Raja walked tall, as pleased as if he had won a prize himself. While she did not have athletic credentials, Veena possessed a stellar academic record. The schoolwork, the intense academic coaching, the dance classes, and the school clubs—the Math Club and the Quiz Club—she handled it all.

Inspired by a neighbor's son, who received an award for volunteering, Raja added weekly visits to a local women's shelter to Veena's list of activities.

He entrusted to Usha the task of going through all the college-related literature that arrived in the mail each day. Every elite institution tried to sell itself. Veena received academic brochures, letters from their presidents, and information about on-campus living.

As far as Raja was concerned, he'd covered all the bases. Usha sensed his anticipation. He saw Harvard beckon.

Inevitably, someone had to create more hours. Usha cut back on her office hours and worked twenty hours a week. She anticipated Raja's, "Why are you giving up?" speech. It never came. His focus had shifted entirely to Veena.

To her surprise, Usha became fascinated as she learned about universities and the admissions process. She lurked on the website, *College Admission Secrets*, trying to ferret out the likelihood of Veena getting into an elite college. She studied up on essays and essay topics, learned about the PSAT scores and how they determined the National Merit Scholarships, about the SAT, the SAT subject tests, and about the Advanced Placement exams. Spending hour after hour on university websites, Usha tried to build the picture of a typical freshman and visualized Veena on those college campuses.

From academics to extra-curricular activities and the test scores, Veena had it all and juggled it all. Usha's head hurt when she saw Veena's wall calendar; activities written out in different colors, listed by hour for each day. The teenager slept at 11:30 P.M. and rose at 5:30 A.M. She'd become the princess of multitasking.

Her multitasking skills extended beyond the realm of academics and extra-curricular activities. A typical teenager, Veena mastered the art of instant messaging while doing homework. She closed chat windows in a flash if Raja or Usha happened to pass by. Earphones hugged her ears like ornaments as she worked on math problems. She sprawled before the television set in the living room and followed a sitcom while studying for a test. She spent time on her cell phone, discussing a friend's heartbreak even as she raced to type a research paper due the next day. Most often, Veena ate absently, her eyes on a book or on the laptop screen.

Usha asked her, "Don't you want to enjoy the peanut balls I made for you? See how wonderfully sweet the jaggery has made them?"

"I am enjoying them."

"Do you have two brains working at the same time? One for schoolwork and another for recognizing and enjoying food? How can you do two things at the same time? You talk to your friends when you are on the computer, you text as you read, you listen to music and study at the same time. *Yenna* confusion!"

"Mom, leave me alone. I'm doing it, am I not?"

Conflicts arose. When Raja saw her on the phone, he'd ask her to hang up and go over test results with him. If he saw her studying in front of the television, he turned the set off and took the remote with him.

The teenager pushed back. She'd grown into a typical young girl, with the same desires and needs as other teenagers, something Raja did not account for. Subtleties escaped him. He didn't realize his daughter had developed the power of independent thinking. The education she received made her more than just a part of her father's grand plan. Ironically, the same education made her think for herself.

When Raja told her she shouldn't waste time by going to the movies with her friends, Veena turned around and reminded him she had great grades. "If you see my grades falling, you can tell me to stop doing other things. I need my friends."

"Why?" Raja asked, not comprehending. "When you go to college, you'll meet a whole new group of friends. Keep your focus."

Usha saw her pushing back and knew it bothered Raja. He thought he'd fashioned a product, but this product was a girl with individuality.

Raja focused on the academic end of things, Usha didn't.

"Remember, your cell phone has to be turned off when you drive. It's not safe to do two things at the same time." Or, "Call when you get to the movie theater."

Usha sensed Raja's anticipation starting March, 2005. Colleges began mailing in their decisions. Veena applied to twelve schools and received acceptances from six. They awaited the major ones with bated breath. Meanwhile, Veena's high school scheduled the graduation ceremony for the 28th of May.

Raja did not predict the final outcome.

On April 1, 2005, Veena came home, and said in a cheery voice, "Can I talk to you guys?"

Usha felt an immediate, unreasonable dread. The cheer in her daughter's voice sounded unnatural, like an actor's voice. When it came to her daughter's emotions her internal radar worked too well. That feeling in the pit of her stomach intensified when Veena asked her and Raja to sit down.

The school counselor had recommended that Veena apply for the coveted Vonn Foundation Scholarship: a merit-based scholarship covering four years of tuition, books, room, and board at the local university for the top five students in the state. She became one of the five.

As a mother, Usha's first reaction was one of pride. Her second reaction was worry. Worry for Raja. Even as her heart swelled, she agonized for her husband whose face grew pale. She placed a hand on his arm to calm him. His muscles tensed.

Usha vacillated, then rose to give her daughter a hug. "Congratulations!"

Raja wouldn't look at his daughter. "Why don't you wait to hear from Harvard, Brown, and Yale?" he said slowly. "You should know pretty soon. Wait for their decisions before you accept this scholarship."

"Because, I want this!" Veena shouted. "I earned this prestige. I worked for this scholarship. I don't want to go to a cold place. I am from Arizona. I have friends here. I want to continue my dance. And I want to go to the women's shelter on the weekends. This is what I want."

What a series of 'I's!

"Then what was the point in all the work we put into researching colleges? Why apply to so many prestigious institutions? Besides, what will you study here? I thought you want to study Biology?

That department is not ranked number one."

"Economics. The department is ranked in the top ten in the nation."

"Economics? What?"

Raja had dreamed of Veena becoming a physician.

He loved her. His love wouldn't let him tell her how disappointed he felt that she'd decided to meander away from the academic and career path he'd chosen for her.

Face drawn, defeated, he picked up his papers and went into the bedroom. Usha didn't clean the kitchen or load the dishwasher. She sat for a while, then turned off the lights and joined him. He lay on his back as he stared at the news on the television set. She knew he didn't absorb the narrative on the screen. When she lay down next to him, he turned and drew her to him, seeking something. She couldn't say, "It's okay. This is good, too." He didn't believe so. At least, not yet. She heard him rub one fidgety foot against another, over and over, before sleep won over her senses.

From then on, Raja immersed himself in work. He did not need to follow his daughter's academic progress any more. He started attending his investment meetings again; as if winning in the financial markets would make up for what he chalked down as a personal loss.

Usha wished Raja could see Veena now. He'd given her the gift of education, of dance, of community spirit, and most of all, the ability to juggle several things at the same time, a necessary trait for a busy lawyer.

Veena completed her bachelor's degree in three years, finishing at the age of twenty-one. She went to law school right after, qualified as a lawyer at twenty-five, and now worked at a local firm.

She'd blossomed because of everything her father did for her.

18

Love and Loss

2007 – 2009

On Tuesday, October 9, 2007, the Dow Jones Industrial Average closed at a peak of 14,164.53. Usha never forgot that day.

As she stood in front of the stove, stirring a pot of *sambar*, she heard Raja come in from the garage, jingling his car keys. His signature announcement. She heard his footfall, light and rapid, on the hardwood floors. His happy steps told her he had a good day.

"The smell of coriander seeds and coconut is heavenly," he said, inhaling deeply as he came up behind her.

He brought with him the odor of the outdoors; a mix of dry heat and air pollutants contrasted with the air-conditioned house. Her heart danced a jig as he looped his arms around her. Interlocking his fingers by her navel, he cushioned her back with his body and looked over her shoulder at the simmering pot. "Hmm… nice!" he said, rubbing his cheek against hers.

She couldn't tell if he meant the *sambar* or her.

Her hand stopped stirring. A moment pulsed before she shifted her weight to her heels and rested against him. She held on to the promise in the embrace. Without turning around, she knew his face held a smile, deep crinkles fanning out from the corners of his eyes.

"Let's go check out Pebble Lake after dinner," he said.

She shifted her weight forward and put an inch of space between his body and hers.

"What? But that's a retirement community!" She turned around.

"I know. But I want to check it out."

"We're not ready for retirement. You're only fifty."

"Didn't you watch the news today? The markets closed at an all-time high. My portfolios are doing well. At this rate, I can retire early, maybe even before I turn sixty."

The day after their daughter announced her college choice, Raja turned his attention to the world of investments, delving into market indices, stocks and bonds with the same fiery intensity he directed at everything else he undertook. He found the stock market on the rebound, a worthy candidate for his all-consuming passion.

"No, I had a busy day at work. No time for the news. Anyway, why do you want to look at property now?"

"Now's as good a time as any!"

"Raja, be serious. You won't know what to do with yourself if you retire. You don't know how to relax."

"I want to move into a gated retirement community, live on the golf course. Or on the lake. Why is that so bad?"

"But you don't play golf!"

"So, I'll learn."

"What about me? I'll only be fifty-three," she giggled. She did that when she anticipated intimacy.

"Well, you can retire, too. Learn how to swim, you never did learn that skill. You can join a book club. Stop quibbling and putting up all these road blocks. The thing is, the stock market is doing well and I'm ready to upgrade, relax, enjoy the fruits of my labor."

Usha supposed she should thank the stock market for taking his attention away from Veena and from herself. When she decided to head Campus Station, the non-profit which helped high school students get into college, he'd only asked, "Do they know you don't have a background in education?"

"Of course," she'd said. "Yet, they offered me the job." She didn't explain she had plenty of hands-on experience with Veena. When the committee found out Veena was a Vonn Foundation Scholar, the job became hers.

After dinner, they drove to Pebble Lake. He marveled at the im-posing entrance to the community—water cascading in mini waterfalls on either side of the entrance gates. The guard at the gate inquired about their business. When they told him they were prospective buyers, he directed them to the sales office. Despite the fading day-light, they saw a wide, palm-tree lined avenue stretching beyond the gate, oleander bushes dotting the center divider. A golf course yawned on one side while a man-made lake shimmered on the oppo-site.

"This is where I want to be," he said. "Exclusive. No unneces-sary people wandering the streets. Everyone accounted for."

She wanted to say, "*We've been perfectly safe without an entrance gate and a guard so far.*" She didn't.

On the way back, they stopped at *Baskin Robbins* and ate ice cream, hers chocolate fudge, his strawberry. They dipped into each other's cups, tongues seduced by mingled flavors.

When they pulled into the garage, he didn't wait to get into the house. Reaching over, he rubbed his thumb over her lips and said, "Come, my dear," as he drew her closer. She'd never been kissed in a car before.

Should I thank the stock market for this?

Other stray thoughts chased one another: dinner dishes in the sink, range speckled with *sambar* drippings, moist clothes struggling to breathe in the washer. She mopped the thoughts quickly and wrung them out of her mind.

This was wild, adventurous, daring even. The blended flavors of chocolate and strawberry lingered, reminding her that this was her husband, this man who made these atypical, amorous advances in his pristine car. He continued kissing her as they went in, forgetting to pull down the garage door for the night, forgetting to brush his teeth, forgetting to change into night clothes. She'd read articles about couples reconnecting after the children left home; for her, it became connecting for the first time, connecting at a primal level. Elemental.

She didn't remember October 9, 2007, and the stock market's high number for the impromptu house hunting expedition or the ice-cream. She remembered it as the night Raja made love to her like never before.

༄

In the months following, he turned inward again, focusing his attention on the stock market which had dropped twenty percent by mid-2008, a major reversal from its highs previous October.

Later, she wondered if she should have questioned his investment policy; asked him if he took profits when things soared or whether he kept buying into every little dip.

What areas do you invest in? Do you concentrate on real estate, or do you buy companies that mine gold, silver and platinum? Do you buy blue-chip companies or do you speculate on smaller growth companies?

It might have helped him to talk things out with someone outside of the world of investments. His investment club members, engulfed in market minutiae, couldn't be objective.

She hadn't asked.

Instead, she made his favorite spinach *kootu* and onion chutney along with a rich *chakra pongal* laced with melted ghee and nuts for dessert. His tongue apparently didn't register or communicate any of the tastes to his brain.

His indifference bothered her. She decided to risk rebuke or criticism. Deliberately, she over-salted the coconut rice the next day. He didn't comment. He dug into the rice with one hand while tapping on his laptop keys with the other. She understood. To him, eating had devolved into a mechanical activity from a sentient one.

Every evening was spent logging into brokerage accounts, studying charts, placing buy or sell orders for the next day. "My NAV," he muttered through clenched teeth, "is not where it should be."

She knew better than to ask him what he meant.

On September 29, 2008, she found out while listening to *National Public Radio* in the car. The news of the stock market's 777 point drop that day dominated the news. Trepidation took root in her belly.

"This unprecedented one-day drop has the investors worried about their net asset values," the market correspondent said.

The phone rang as she walked into the house. Raja, she thought, lunging for the phone.

"Hello!" Veena said.

"Oh, hi, Veena! How are your classes?" she asked.

"Fine. Everything's fine. Where's Dad? I haven't talked to him in days. He didn't answer his cell phone either."

"He's fine. Just busy with work. He's not back yet. Probably went to his investment club meeting after work."

"Don't tell me he's still with that old bunch! The market fell today. If I were him, I'd put my money under the mattress instead of the stock market."

"Don't say things like that. He knows what he is doing, markets go down and then they do go up. It will be fine."

Raja didn't come home until late. He called, distracted, around 7:30 P.M. "The group is re-vamping investment strategy. You must have heard the news. Don't stay up."

"Yes, it's on every channel," she told him. She didn't remind him about dinner. He'd stopped caring about food.

Until that big plunge, the Dow Jones Industrial Average, as a number, meant nothing. After that, it became a number with meaning, one that controlled the atmosphere in their house.

Things got worse. Raja withdrew farther into his world of numbers. He couldn't take defeat; instead, he tried to manipulate their accounts. She watched as he buried himself in his computer and attempted to find sectors where he could find returns.

Deep lines made semi-circular arches on either side of his mouth. He'd long forgotten to lift it in a smile. His eyebrows grew gray overnight. Although his preoccupation allowed him to eat little, he gathered weight around his middle. He slept late but woke early, obsessed with catching the futures numbers before the markets opened.

Still, he couldn't control market forces, nor could he preempt disaster.

On January 20, 2009, the market closed at 7,949. She absorbed the number, stunned.

On October 9, 2007, the market had closed at over 14,164. And now this? Aren't the numbers supposed to move in the opposite direction?

For the first time in her married life, she worried about their financial situation. She wished she had paid attention to all those brokerage accounts. She wondered how much he had put into the stock market.

Perhaps he is depleting our retirement accounts as well?

A question knocked.

What would have happened if Veena didn't have a scholarship?

Thankfully, they had no commitment to a private school with its hefty tuition. On the other hand, paying for college could have prevented Raja's plunge into the market.

When problems occupied Raja's mind, he tended to become silent, withdrawing like a tortoise into its shell. Everything about him shouted, "Don't ask me anything." Repeated questions about his wellbeing angered him.

He didn't like failure. But the financial market, his capricious mistress, refused to cooperate.

༄

She received the call at work.

"Hi, this is Richard Hoskins," a man said, his address familiar as if she should know him. "Please don't get worried. Your husband has taken ill and we took him to Jefferson."

For a moment she didn't understand. She couldn't place him. Richard? Richard. Oh yes, the man with the glamorous and high-achieving Cindy for a wife.

A vague premonition found a home under her diaphragm.

What did Richard say? Raja has taken ill. But he was fine when he left for work this morning.

"Hello?" Richard said. "Are you there?"

"Yes, yes, sorry. I'm trying to grasp this. Raja is ill? What happened?"

"It would be best if you came to Jefferson Hospital. Come to Emergency."

"Okay. I'll be there in a few minutes."

She grabbed her bag, shouted out to Patricia that she had an emergency, took the steps down two at a time and ran to her car. She couldn't get her key into the ignition to start the car.

Richard's calm words, pitched low, did not sound panicked.

She buckled her seat belt.

This can't be serious.

Raja worried a lot lately, but didn't fall ill. Like most men she knew, he didn't like to visit the doctor. The last time he went a physician, ten years ago, he had had a serious attack of influenza. Even then she had to battle his reluctance, force him into the doctor's office, and coax him to take the antibiotics. Faithfully, she subjected herself to yearly check-ups, but could not persuade him. When asked, he'd laugh and say, "Nothing's broken, why bother to find out if something's wrong?" He didn't know his cholesterol numbers, if his blood sugar was high, or where his blood pressure stood.

It took her longer to find parking than it did to get to the hospital. She sped into Emergency where Richard waited. He didn't look her in the eye; instead, he stepped forward and put his hand on her shoulder. His touch told her what words could not.

Someone sat her down in a chair, some faceless doctor made sympathetic noises, and someone else called Veena and Marcy. "We did everything we possibly could for your husband. Unfortunately, his heart gave out," boomed in her head.

She didn't cry. She absorbed the news in the midst of all the busyness around her, all the noise. Veena would come soon. So would Marcy. A hollowness gaped inside, an emptiness as if someone had taken a ladle and scooped out everything.

She wished she could shut out the noise, turn off the television mounted on the wall in front of her. A number flashed on the screen. The Dow Jones Industrial Average closed at 6,443.27 that day.

A flash and she knew.

In the end, the attribute that defined Raja— his pursuit of excellence—became his undoing. He died on March 6, 2009, the day the markets hit bottom, without achieving his immigrant's dream.

19

Emotional Distance

July 29 – 30, 2012

S unday night, when she got the house to herself, Usha
went on a sweet binge.

She didn't protest when Veena offered to drop Marcy
off at the airport. Her friend dispatched affectionate glances her way
and rubbed her head as if she were a child. Such benevolence irked
her. She endured Marcy's long hug as she said good-bye; it would
seem churlish not to.

Her daughter hovered, attentive, as if an innate sense told her
something. "Did you want me to come back here tonight instead of
going to my apartment?" She offered to clear the dishwasher, do
laundry, or water the rose bushes in the yard. Uncharacteristically, she
even put away her indispensable cell phone and ignored all other
electronic devices.

"Stop it," Usha wanted to shout. *"Arjay's scheming doesn't deserve so much attention."* Of course, they couldn't know about it.

She wore a calm mask. "Veena, I'm fine. I'm sure you have things to do. If I need you, I'll call."

For once, she forgot to remind Veena not to answer her phone while driving. Even before Veena's car left the driveway, Usha reached for her salve. She pulled out a treat from the freezer—mango ice-cream—and settled down in front of the television. Nothing captured her interest.

There is always YouTube with its stock of British sitcoms.

She'd become addicted to *Yes, Minister* and *Yes, Prime Minister* which had aired on Indian television a long time ago. In the late eighties, she'd discovered the Public Broadcasting System in the United States and shows like *Good Neighbors*, *'Allo 'Allo*, and *Keeping Up Appearances*. She rearranged the pillows on her bed so she could rest comfortably against the headboard. With her laptop and with dessert, she got ready for an evening of British comedy.

Her cell phone rang. She turned it off without looking to see who called. Arjay didn't know her home number so he couldn't call the landline.

He can wait at the restaurant. Wait and wait.

While watching episodes of *Good Neighbors*, she licked clean the container of mango ice-cream. The sweet fulfilled her with a level of satiety that no meal could provide. At 11:00 P.M., she decided it was too early to go to bed. Time for Mrs. Hyacinth Bucket on *Keeping Up Appearances*.

She hit pause on the computer, padded to the refrigerator, and found the walnut-covered brownies she'd taken into work last week. Thankfully, she'd brought back the leftovers.

She fell asleep sitting up against her headboard. The laptop, still on, slid off her lap onto the bed.

She woke up Monday morning, her head heavy and eyes struggling to open. She rubbed her elbow and knee joints, hoping to lubricate her body and encourage it to move. It ached as if she were heading for a bout of the summer flu. Temptation lured her sleepward, told her to forget about work. She sluiced her face with cold water and rubbed the sleep away from her eyes.

The home phone rang as Usha picked up her bag to leave for work. She debated for a second—it could be Veena, or even Marcy, and her cell phone was off—then picked it up.

"Hi, Usha? Anu here. How are you?"

Usha rubbed her forehead as she tried to place Anu. Memory nudged her into recognition. Of course, a friend from her undergraduate days. Anu lived in India. They hadn't spoken in a few years. She ought to express happiness, an old friend was reaching out; yet she felt an empty distance, both physical and emotional.

Not a particularly good day for this call.

"Hello, Anu. Where are you calling from?"

"I'm visiting my daughter in Seattle. Didn't you get her wedding invitation two years ago? She's pregnant and I'm here to help."

Usha didn't remember the invitation. She didn't recall a lot of things from two years ago. Besides, her brain had lost its sharpness this morning.

"Oh, that's nice." Trite, but she found a response.

"So tell me, how are you?"

"I'm fine. And you?"

"Just waiting for the baby, you know. They've gone off to work, my daughter and son-in-law, so I thought I'd call my old friends who live in the States. How is Veena? Married?"

"No, Veena's not married." She braced herself for the next question. No matter how many times she'd been through this, she couldn't diminish the distress for both parties.

"And Raja? Still as busy as ever? You guys should stay with us when you come to India next. We're also free now, children all gone."

Usha recognized the needles of impending tears, took a deep breath. Although too tired for this conversation, she found no easy way around it. "Raja passed away three years ago, Anu."

Anu's shock transmitted through the phone line. "Oh! Oh, no. I am so sorry!"

At this point, as with similar conversations in the past, the exchange grew awkward. She couldn't say, "It's okay;" she didn't like the falsehood. She could simply say, "Thank you," but to her that sounded cold, clinical. Her lack of sleep and confused mental state made her want to wallow, to weep and weep. On the other hand, she wanted to end the phone call.

"I've had some time to deal with it."

Anu remained stuck on the "I'm so sorry" part. She repeated it twice more.

"Thanks for calling, Anu. But I'm running late for work."

"Work?"

Anu must think I stopped working when Raja died. Should I tell her he died on a Friday, and I was back at work on Monday?

She'd squeezed everything into that one weekend which culminated with the cremation on Sunday. Action became her panacea; she couldn't have borne one more day at home.

Now, as she did then, she needed the solace of work, a place to put her thoughts and her focus. "Yes, I'm about to leave. Give me your number and I'll call you back some other time."

Again, her friend said, "I'm so sorry." This time, for calling at an inappropriate hour. She rattled off her contact number in an apparent hurry to hang up the phone.

Usha sensed she wouldn't hear from her again.

20

The Surgical Cut

July 30, 2012

Usha negotiated the morning rush hour, wishing she hadn't picked up the phone, wishing her friend hadn't called. All this talk of death coming on the heels of Arjay's shenanigans brought with it a reminder of her vulnerability.

After the devastating blow it dealt her, death forced her to deal with the enormity of the unfinished business left behind and the tangible loss.

Most people around her hadn't known how to handle the news of Raja's untimely death. Many stayed away, not because they didn't empathize. Quite the contrary. They probably felt awful, so perturbed, they didn't know what to say or how to say it. Even in her sorrow, she understood their quandary.

A few sent cards, as if it was easier not to meet her in person. Others brought food and didn't speak, their silent presence intended to convey sympathy.

Those closest to her, however—Marcy, and the girls at work—held her hand, listened, and told her they'd be there for her in the days to come; all she had to do was call and they'd be there. No one understood the gnawing void that remained after everyone returned to their daily routines, to their loved ones. They had lives to lead while hers felt like it had ground to a stop.

When her parents died, one after the other, ten years ago, she had expected their demise. They'd both been in ill-health for a long time. Besides, they had lived long, fruitful lives, and, more importantly, she'd been back several times to see them before they died. Raja's death stunned with its abruptness. So staggering, Mr. Param—Raja's father—died a month later of a heart attack. Raja's mother, the voluble Mrs. Param, retreated into uncharacteristic silence and refused to communicate with Usha.

༺༻

At work, she logged on to her computer. Four emails from Arjay greeted her. She squeezed her eyes shut and told herself this weepiness must stop or she couldn't get through the day.

Of course, he'll contact me.

The first email said, "Are you okay?" on the subject line. Another one asked, "Where are you?" A third said, "Why aren't you answering the phone?" And the last message, "Please call me."

She deleted all four. Her cell phone probably held a few text messages from him. She hadn't bothered to turn her phone on since last evening. This cut demanded to be surgical.

He didn't know she knew. He didn't know the gig was up.

Or will he guess?

He saw her profile on the website and decided to stalk her. For a moment, she wondered if she should confront him and get the weight off her chest.

"Scoundrel! Rogue!" she'd yell at him. *"I know what you've done. How many women have you lassoed like this? With your superficial niceties? Did you honestly think I would never find out? How long did you think you could continue fooling me?"*

She wanted to make the color drain from his face with the shock of her unexpected attack. She wanted to make him squirm.

And a voice whispered. *To what purpose?*

Rubbing her temples, she turned off her monitor. Of course, it would help to release her festering anger and give her the satisfaction of telling him off. However, the final result could be no different.

But I can slap him. Roar at him. A bitter laugh shook her chest. She knew she was kidding herself. All of those reactions were some-one else's, not hers.

Rosa knocked on the door. "We're ready for our status meeting," she said.

"Be there in a minute," Usha replied. She printed out the agenda for the meeting and picked up a yellow marker. It reminded her of Arjay and his highlighted books. She'd stolen a look at one of his tomes in the coffee shop. He had to go through boxes and boxes of markers. His vivid highlighting had drawn her eyes to the marked passages. "Stop it," she whispered, dropping the yellow coloring pen into the trash receptacle under her desk.

A cup of coffee waited by her designated seat. Heather knew how she liked her coffee: two teaspoons of sugar, milky. "Thanks, Heather," she said, grateful for the caffeine. She needed it to find her focus today. Neither her body nor her mind wanted to function.

Everyone else discussed the weather. Rosa and Lisa complained about traveling to schools in the heat.

"The monsoon season supposedly peaks between mid-July and mid-August, but here it is, almost the beginning of August and not a cloud in sight," Lisa said.

"After those short-lived thunderstorms weeks ago, we've had nothing. Anyway, most times we only get dust storms. I don't know which is worse, the heat or the dust," Rosa said.

"Stop whining, ladies. We know the statistics, about eight inches of rain a year. So, why hope for more?" Heather, the serious one, said. "To change the subject... On Friday, we have Canyon State reps coming here. They'll bring their new fall catalogs, brochures, on-campus housing information, and stuff like that. Six students have signed up to talk to them. I need help."

"I'm here and I can help," Lisa said.

Usha allowed the discussion to eddy around her while she waited for the coffee to send her some clarity of thought.

"Usha, phone call on line two," Patricia called from the reception desk.

"Who is it?"

"Someone from Valley University."

She had expected this. Of course. If Arjay couldn't reach her via cell phone or email, this would become the logical next step.

"Take a message. I'm in a meeting." She took a sip of coffee, hoping to return her focus to the meeting.

Mid-morning, Patricia buzzed her to say Veena was on the line. "Are you okay, Mother? You seemed upset yesterday. Was it the website? I've been trying you all day."

"Oh, my ringer's off. Don't worry, Veena. I'm okay."

A hollowness in the phone line alerted her. "Veena, Veena?" The call had dropped.

The phone rang again, immediately.

"Veena, are you driving? I've told you not to call anyone when you're driving."

"Mother, it's hands-free."

"Still, it's a distraction. I hope you don't check your text messages when you drive?"

"Jeez! And I thought I'd check on you. Just stop with this lecturing. I've got things under control. By the way, Masyma's left you messages."

"I'm fine. I'll send Marcy an email right away and I'll call you in the evening."

Moments pulsed as if Veena was in thought. Then, she said, "Okay," and hung up the phone.

Usha knew her daughter worried.

How much does she know about Arjay? At the moment, there is nothing to tell. Nothing at all.

After lunch, she pushed personal thoughts away and became engrossed in Campus Station's financial columns. She faced a deficit this year. While the economy had turned the corner, their benefactors, still recovering, withheld generosity. Campus Station needed corporate partnerships to run the office: to buy supplies, arrange workshops, get speakers, and employ the five of them. The shortfall worried her. She tapped numbers into her calculator.

Patricia knocked.

"A young man to see you," she said. "Can I send him in?"

"A student?"

She nodded.

Usha pressed her knuckles against her forehead. Her headache wouldn't go away. "Why does he want to see me? Isn't Heather around? I know Rosa and Lisa are out."

"He says he's met you before."

"What's his name? Oh well, send him in."

She pushed her papers away and turned the monitor off.

A hesitant knock on the door.

Andres.

She bit her lip.

Not today.

He wore the white shirt with blue jeans again. In his hands, he held a glass jar with a red ribbon tied around its neck.

"Good afternoon!"

"Hello," she forced a smile. "How can I help you?"

"I wanted to talk to you about my scholarship essays. Would you take a look at them for me?"

Andres reminded her of Arjay and her visit to Valley University. She tapped random numbers into the calculator. When she looked up, he still stood by the door. "I'm in the middle of something right now. This is not a good time."

Andres' face fell. "Okay. Please, can I have an appointment?"

Usha sighed. "I don't know. Let me see when I'm free."

Why am I punishing him for something Arjay did?

She checked her calendar and ran a quick look at her appointments for the next few days. "How about three o'clock on Friday?"

"Thank you!" He cleared his throat. "My mom, like... umm... wanted me to give you this."

He gave her the jar he held in his hands.

"For me? Why?"

Andres rubbed the blunt edges of his fingernails with his thumb as if he was ready to pick one of them to chew on. "Because you're helping me. You gave me that list of scholarships last time. No one in our family has been to college, in like, ever. It's a big deal. My mom said she hopes you like homemade salsa."

She fingered the red ribbon and untied the bow. She changed her mind and knotted the bow again. Her throat swelled up. All day the tears lingered, threatening to spill at the slightest provocation.

"Tell her I said thank you. Now, about the universities. Local universities start accepting applications in September. So let's go over what you need to do when you get here on Friday. Maybe you can polish those scholarship essays until then?"

"Thank you." Andres' eyes shone with hope as he left.

His best bet would be to get a complete tuition waiver based on merit. She'd already spoken with Arjay. He'd mentioned the consortium. She should give this boy his email address and phone number.

The cut from Arjay couldn't be as surgical as she'd like it to be.

21

Second Thoughts

August 3, 2012

*U*sha flung the dog-eared, much-flipped-through magazine on the chair next to her. The stream of music blasting from the overhead speakers at the auto service center annoyed her. To give herself something to do, she picked up yet another drink from the little refrigerator in the waiting room. At 2:00 P.M, she decided she'd had enough. She went up to the customer window and asked about her vehicle a third time. Raja had taken care of car maintenance; he kept meticulous service records. He hadn't told her auto mechanics tended to swindle women by adding unnecessary repairs. This time, again, the mechanic found problems with the vehicle when she asked for a simple oil change.

A spike shot through her. This happened often these days, unexpected moments when Raja made her angry. Never when they were

162

married. Then, she'd focused on orchestrating peace, as if expressions of annoyance might cause the balance to teeter.

"So, umm...," she peered at the name tag on the man's shirt, "Tom, what's going on? You told me if I brought my car in at noon, it would be ready in forty-five minutes. I've been here for two hours and still no car."

"Sorry ma'am, we're short-staffed today. We usually are in the summer. Some of our guys decide to take long weekends or they go to Flagstaff to cool off."

"So, you should have asked me to come another day."

He continued, "And you know we also had to replace your brake pads, rotate your tires, plus the oil change. I'm sure it'll be soon now. Let me check."

She kicked herself for agreeing to all those extras. "I can't wait any longer. I have to get back to work."

He made a couple of calls. "We can give you a ride back to work. I'll call when your car's ready."

"You couldn't have told me this when I came in at noon?" She clenched her teeth to conserve the rest of her words and glared at him.

In two minutes, a van appeared to take her back to work.

∞

She checked her emails one last time before the meeting with Andres. No new messages from Arjay. One remained from yesterday. She erased it.

He had gathered her intent.

So, this is how a burgeoning relationship in the modern world forms and breaks off, no more than a floating game.

She lacked the skills for these new times. She should never have entered the arena.

A burning sensation grew at her sternum. It had to be the spicy burrito she swallowed at lunchtime. She pressed her fingers against her chest. While waiting for her car, she'd read in a health magazine that stress aggravated heartburn. Taking a sip of water, she stood. She didn't have the time deal with her stress issues in the middle of the afternoon on a work day.

As she headed toward the front desk to tell Patricia she expected Andres, he walked in.

"You're prompt," she said. "That's good. Come with me."

"Hold on, young man, sign here, please." Patricia extended a clipboard toward him.

Andres stepped forward to the desk.

Usha's skin detected a slender lift of space and with it, a presence. She sensed a charge in the atmosphere. Although she didn't face the main door, she knew it had opened. Her practical brain convinced her that the senses only captured the movement of air, that the nose identified the scent of someone else's lingering aftershave.

A burning at her breastbone again.

She knew.

"Hello, Usha!" Arjay said. That's all. No more.

Why is he here?

She turned and offered a perfunctory greeting.

His tired eyes with puffy bags spoke of things unsaid. She had an urge to run her finger under each eye and to press the swelling back.

Perhaps I could have handled the Sunday situation a little better.

She'd stood Arjay up. He had a reservation at the romantic Cafe 360 Degrees, the revolving restaurant with breathtaking views of the city. She hadn't bothered to call and cancel.

How long did he wait at that table? Perhaps he ordered a drink and then an appetizer while he waited.

At some point, he'd have asked for the bill and tried to avoid the waiter's sympathetic glances. As he left, he might have noticed a couple in hushed conversation, holding hands across their table.

Did he have his head down as he left; did his shoulders droop?

She shut the inner voice down and allowed her anger to surface once again. He created this situation, no reason for her to feel guilty. When they'd met, he'd known who she was and he didn't tell her. He didn't bother to mention he recognized her from the dating website. His actions impelled her withdrawal. The only things she'd accept blame for, her inexperience and her naiveté.

How often have I wished to find a flaw in this man?

She'd found it. His unnatural steadiness annoyed her. For once, she appreciated Raja and his unbridled expressions of annoyance, anger, and frustration. She'd known exactly where she stood with him. She could do without Arjay's control, his composure, and his politeness.

How she wished she could release some of the disappointment building all this pressure inside. She gulped down words. So much to say.

Not now. If he wears the mask of formality, so can I.

Click, click, click. She pursed her lips. Her mind calculated. Andres. Valley University. And here he was, Arjay Wheeler, the very man to help Andres. Opportune perhaps.

"Oh, hello!" With effort, Usha excavated professionalism from inner reserves. "Come, Arjay, let's go to our meeting area."

Arjay's eyebrows rose. Deep, horizontal creases appeared on his forehead. "What?" he asked. He recovered in an instant and followed her with an, "Okay."

She found Heather and Lisa cleaning up.

"Give us a minute," Heather said. Usha tapped her foot as they rearranged chairs and picked up balled up papers. Arjay and Andres hovered outside the door.

"The weatherman on the radio gave a forecast of 98 degrees for today," Heather said. Today, nature decided to bestow one of her rare gifts in the middle of summer, sousing Phoenix with a ten-degree temperature drop. Moods lightened with the drop in temperature.

"We're strange," Lisa said. "Only Phoenicians would think 98 degrees is great."

"You forget, my dear, it's down more than twelve degrees since yesterday," Heather said. "Besides, as they say, it's a dry heat! So we don't sweat as much."

"Heather, Lisa," Usha interrupted their conversation. She gestured to Arjay and Andres, indicating they should come in as well. "Meet Dr. Arjay Wheeler from Valley University. That's A-R-J-A-Y. Funny, I thought his name was the initial R and the initial J when I met him first." She talked too much, a response to stress.

"You're right, Usha. My name did come from the initials. My parents couldn't decide whether to name me Robert or John, for my grandfather or my great grandfather. Hence, Arjay."

"It's nice to meet you, Dr. Wheeler. I'm sure you'll be hearing from us." Heather shook hands with him.

"Sorry, Usha, we were clearing up after those Canyon State reps. They had a good session today," Lisa said.

"By the way, this is Andres. He's interested in Valley University. Heather, I might ask him to work with you," Usha said.

"Hey, Andres! Contact me anytime. Happy to help," Heather said.

She left with Lisa.

Andres and Arjay found two seats at the table while Usha went to fetch bottles of water. She handed Arjay his cold bottle and refused to make eye contact. His fingers brushed hers. She pulled her hand away as if she'd touched a hot pan.

She opened her bottle, took a swig, and felt the cool water hit the burning spot under her breastbone. "So, Andres, I know we were supposed to go over some other things today," she said. "But you're fortunate to have Dr. Wheeler here. He is the Director of Admissions for Valley University. It would be a good idea to ask him questions about scholarships and the admissions process. Did you bring your transcripts and scores?"

Andres nodded as he chewed on what remained of the nail on his thumb.

"Andres has excellent SAT scores, besides which he is in the top five percent of his class." Usha patted the student on his shoulder, hoping to put the young man at ease. She rose. "I'll be in my office. Why don't the two of you talk?"

"It would be best if you stayed, Usha."

She narrowed her eyes. It didn't help her read his expression. She shook her head. "Why? You can tell him all about your university. I don't need to be here."

"You do, to make it an official discussion. Remember, I'm in your office not mine."

Does he enjoy making things complex? There can never be any trust between us, he must know that. Why is he here anyway? Perhaps he is here to bring it all out in the open, have a good, old-fashioned show-down. That's how Raja would have handled the situation.

Not Arjay.

"Usha, urgent phone call for you," Patricia shrieked.

Patricia, don't shout in the office.

She picked up the nearest extension. "This is Usha," she said.

"Amma," Veena quavered. As a baby, she'd called her Amma in keeping with the Indian tradition. In elementary school, that morphed to Mommy, which then became shortened to Mom when Veena went into high school. Lately, Veena called her Mother, infusing the decorum of adulthood.

167

Usha's body responded to the quaver before the brain did. She put her fingers to her mouth. The threat of spicy regurgitation returned. "What is it? What is it?" she whispered.

"Don't freak out, okay? Maybe you should sit down first."

"Sit? Why?" Usha yelled.

"Calm down. I had an accident."

"A car accident?" she shouted. A moment ago she had accused Patricia of doing the same thing. A visual formed in her brain: Veena on the phone, distracted, her gaze averted from the road for a second as a big black truck slammed right into the driver's side window. Over and over again, she had asked her daughter to turn the phone's ringer off while driving. Veena had heard the warning from her for many, many years. "Oh, no, no. What? How? Where are you? Are you hurt? Hold on, baby, I'll be there as quickly as I can."

"I'm okay; I'm okay. Listen, I'm okay. But my car…"

She had no time to waste. "Quickly, where are you?"

"Corner of 22nd Street and Camelback. You know, by the Gilmore."

"Ten minutes. I'll be there, okay, sweetie? Hang on."

Usha closed her eyes and summoned strength. She repeated to herself, "Veena is okay."

"Sorry, I have to leave." She flung the words at Arjay and Andres before she ran into her office and grabbed her bag. At the front desk, she stopped a second. "Patricia, if anyone asks, I had to run. My daughter's been in a car accident." She clattered down the stairs without waiting for a response.

Shivers careened through her. Three years ago, she'd run out of the office just like this. Her life had altered after that phone call. It hadn't occurred to her to ask questions then. She'd believed then that Raja was fine; ill, but fine; certainly not at death's door.

Logic urged, told her things were different this time. This time, she'd spoken to Veena who told her only the car sustained damages.

Someone materialized at her side.

Arjay said, "Wait here, I'll get my car."

"No," she shouted. "Please. I can get to my daughter."

He placed a hand on her shoulder, looked into her eyes. "It's safer this way."

She wanted to push him away.

Does he imagine I'll fall for him if he acts like my knight in shining armor? Those things only happen in romances.

She'd read many before she married Raja. In a rush, she remembered. She didn't have her car. Of all days. She balled her fists. "Okay," she mumbled.

He brought his car around. She got in and said, "Corner of 22nd Street and Camelback." After a pause, she continued, "And thank you, for doing this. I appreciate it."

He touched her hand. "You're welcome. This happened to me. My wife. I... at that time, I wasn't available. I couldn't possibly stay away now."

An image arose of the woman in the photograph at his house. Marcy had tried to press him about the lady with the serene smile. He'd ushered them away. That woman had died in a car crash. He didn't talk about it then. She died.

Oh God, let Veena be fine.

No time. There was no time to think of photographs and serene smiles.

Her heart jumped as the car lurched. She noticed he pressed his foot to the pedal. Not something she'd have expected from someone who did everything in such a controlled manner.

"If a cop wants to give me a speeding ticket, he can follow me to the site of the accident," he said, following the direction of her gaze.

22

The Accident

August 3, 2012

A rjay screeched to a halt.

Heart pounding, Usha took in the surreal scene which looked like a still from a movie. Traffic trickled, reduced to one slow lane as a result of the accident. Curious drivers from passing cars checked out the damage as they drove past. The lights of a police car flashed and a fire truck's engine hummed.

At the intersection, Veena's red car stood askew, driver's side door hanging open. Strewn bits of broken glass on the ground reflected sunlight. The vehicle that crashed into her, an older model judging from the chipped paint on the roof, was situated awkwardly, its nose almost buried into the front of Veena's car. As if it were hallowed ground, an invisible circle had been circumscribed around the immediate area, people and cars staying a respectful distance away.

She shuddered a breath. Veena stood at the northwest corner, talking to a policeman. Her daughter was able to stand, to talk.

She must be okay.

Usha lunged out of the car, ran to Veena, and put her arms around her. She leaned back to take a look at her face. "Are you okay? Anything broken?"

"Don't worry, Mother. I'm fine." Veena smiled, an offering of strength.

"Your nose looks swollen and red. I'm concerned."

"Mother," Veena rolled her eyes, indicating she should stop the fuss. "This is Officer Galway. He's been very kind."

Relief rippled through Usha. Veena had pulled herself together. Her voice lost the quaver Usha detected over the phone.

"Officer, what happened? Who's the irresponsible lout that hit my daughter?"

"Ah, lady, lady!" the officer chuckled. "Such faith your daughter is not at fault? Well, there's the lout that hit your daughter."

A woman sat at the curb, her gray head in her hands.

"That's her? But she must be at least eighty years old! Poor thing, she looks sad!"

"Yep. She's waiting for her son. Your daughter and she have exchanged insurance information and phone numbers. No one's seriously hurt, so the EMTs can leave. And here's the tow truck now to take your daughter's car away."

Usha turned to look at Veena's car and clapped a hand to her mouth. She absorbed the fender hanging loose, the missing headlight, and the crumpled folds of the car's hood.

"What exactly happened?" She thought she detected a quiver in Veena's nostrils. She added, "Would you rather not talk about it?"

"No, it's fine. I had a left arrow and I was about to turn when she hit me head on." Veena's eyes narrowed. "Hey," she yelled, "what the heck do you think you're doing?"

Usha pulled on her daughter's arm. Her ears burned. "Veena, that's Dr. Wheeler. He brought me here."

He held up his palm, indicating they should hold on.

"Who?"

"Dr. Arjay Wheeler."

"What? Why? Wow!"

Usha's maternal radar flipped itself on. The built-in mechanism sent out a series of beeps. She couldn't decide whether Veena's questions indicated curiosity or annoyance. "Well, it's a long—"

"What happened to your car?"

"It's getting an oil change."

"*Ai, yai, yai!* Can this day get any crazier?"

Arjay put Veena's laptop, her bag, and sundry papers from her car into his, then came over. "Sorry. I wanted to clear the car before the tow truck took it away. It's not a good idea to leave anything personal in there." He stretched his hand out. "Hello, I'm Arjay Wheeler."

Tongue-tied for a brief moment, Veena blinked twice and smiled. A slow flush crept over her face. Her efficient, business-like persona went into hiding.

Is my daughter embarrassed?

When Arjay touched her hand, Veena said, "Ouch," and pulled it away.

"I think that needs to be looked at," he said. "Where's the nearest emergency room? St. Mary's?"

"I'm fine, really."

"He's right," Usha said. "I don't like the swelling on your nose either. Why don't we check both out?"

"Don't make a big deal, Mother! I'm supposed to be at a meeting. What I need is a rental car. I really don't have time for the emergency room."

Veena turned to Arjay. "Sorry about all this."

"We must have you looked at," Usha insisted. "Don't worry about a rental car." Words lodged in her throat, and she cleared it to move them along. "You can take Dad's car if there's any problem with the insurance people." She hadn't sold Raja's car. Occasionally, she drove it to work.

"I'll drive you to the hospital," Arjay said.

Rubbing her throat, she said, "Thanks. We're taking too much of your time."

"Not a problem."

Little conversation in the car. Usha wondered if Veena sat seething in the back seat. Her daughter hated others making decisions for her. She sneaked a look in the mirror on her visor. Veena's attention lay buried in her phone—the instrument her daughter's passport to sullen retreat.

She rubbed her temples where a headache lurked. Her radar detected mixed signals from Veena: curiosity, interest, embarrassment, and finally, this withdrawal.

"Thank you for the ride. So nice to meet you," Veena said when they got to the hospital. She picked up the bedraggled cloth grocery bag with the odds and ends Arjay had gathered from her car.

Veena, don't dismiss him like that.

Another thought bloomed.

I'm a fine one to chastise my daughter.

"I mean, we don't know how long we'll be here." Veena brought back lost politeness.

"Yes, thank you for everything. Really, we've imposed too much," Usha added.

"I'll stay and take you back."

Usha could have said one of the girls at work would be happy to give them a ride. She didn't.

His wife had died in a car crash. He was unavailable when the accident had occurred.

Do his actions now help to assuage his grief, his guilt?

Usha had refused to answer his emails, his texts or his phone calls over the last few days. He did not appear take umbrage. He hadn't acknowledged her behavior.

A strategy to kill me with kindness?

She shushed the voice.

At the desk, inattentive hospital staff assured Veena she'd receive prompt attention. A promise Usha knew they could not fulfill; patients milled around the waiting area.

They settled into the only available chairs in the back. Veena focused her gaze on the front desk, willing the staff to call her name next. Usha stared at the television screen mounted on the wall in front. The evening news began. Veena's phone dinged.

5:30 P.M. Usha jumped up. Her plastic chair tipped over. "The service center closes at six," she said.

"What service center?" Arjay righted her chair.

"My car is at the auto service place. I dropped it off this morning for an oil change and I was supposed to pick it up later in the afternoon. With everything that happened, I forgot."

If he wondered why she'd protested so vehemently when he told her he'd drive her to the scene of the accident, he didn't reveal it. "I'll take you."

"I'm so sorry for the trouble."

How many times have I apologized to him already? Yet, his lapse remains unmentioned.

Veena, in the middle of a text, concentrated on her phone.

"I have to get my car. I'll be right back. Will you be okay?"

Her daughter's lips lifted in a sardonic grin. "I'll probably still be in this chair when you get back. Go, get your car. I won't disappear."

"Bye, Veena," Arjay said.

She answered with an absent nod.

23

The Ritual of Formality

August 3, 2012

I n Arjay's car, Usha fumbled for the seatbelt, which disappeared beyond her reach. The search kept thoughts at bay.
She couldn't understand her awkwardness and her self-
consciousness. Neither did she want to analyze them now.

"Where to?" he asked. "Where's your car?"

"Sorry. Should've told you. The auto place is not too far. Just
take Central up to Northern."

"Will your car be ready?"

"It should be. They may have called the office, but you know…"

Silence.

Thoughts crowded the car, suffocating in the confined space.

Perhaps I can open my window a crack to release some of them.

She crossed and uncrossed her legs, feeling the unshaven prickliness. Too tired last night, she pushed away the chore as she showered. She stole a look.

They don't look hairy.

Her skirt fell below the knees; she didn't wear anything shorter. This allowed her to shave from the knees down. She chided herself.

Hardly the time to dwell on hairy legs.

Her feet hurt. The footwear constricted her toes. Every now and then, her feet swelled up, stretching the straps of her sensible two-inch high sandals. She wished she could remove them, give her toes a comforting wiggle.

She had to say something. He looked straight ahead and concentrated on driving.

"I'm sorry." Another apology. Immediately, she realized he might think she offered the regret for not showing up for dinner on Sunday. "I mean about all of this, for the trouble."

"No trouble at all." He didn't smile. With sunglasses protecting his eyes, she couldn't read his expression.

"Thank you."

His turn. But he said nothing.

Now what?

She blinked against the brightness outside.

Where are my sunglasses?

She opened her handbag, stuck a hand in, and rummaged. Summer days in Phoenix tended to be long, dazzling, and hot. The sun wouldn't set until 7:30 P.M at least. She ran a distracted hand over her hair.

I wonder how long I've been walking around with sunglasses perched on my head.

Even the ritual of formality was acceptable, she decided. Otherwise, the unsaid took over. They sat close, the shoulders barely a foot apart in the small car. She smelled the heat his body emanated, caught the whiff of stale deodorant and woodsy aftershave mingled with sweat. On their hike, she fervently told Marcy she couldn't get used to another man; Raja's unique body chemistry had become so much a part of her senses.

Can I get used to another?

Arjay's cotton shirt, probably ironed when he put it on this morning, crumpled now. She saw the crisscross of lines on his back, transferred from some chair he'd leaned against.

"Okay, so I'm almost at Northern. Do I go left or right here?"

She hurried to answer his question. This kind of conversation she could handle. She told him to turn left and to look for the auto service place about a mile down the road on the right.

She noted the changes in his conduct. When he took her to the accident scene, his demeanor was serious and concerned. When he noticed Veena's injury, he suggested they go to the emergency room. Now that things were under control, he became someone else. Distant and formal.

He slowed as he pulled into the auto service center. She looked at the clock on the car's dashboard. It read 5:45.

"There's my car." She pointed to her car parked outside the service entrance, washed and presumably ready to go. "Looks ready. Thanks again for the ride."

Her phone buzzed in her bag.

"Usha?" He turned to look at her.

She couldn't escape when he said her name like that: intimate, grave, laden.

He's been so helpful, I can't say, "Not now, later."

"Yes?" She let the phone ring.

"I called Marcy. That's probably her."

"Marcy? Why? Why did you do that?"

"I called her when I was cleaning out Veena's car. I thought she should know about the accident."

"But how?"

"How did I have her contact number?" He had an uncanny ability to read her mind. "She gave me her card, remember?"

Marcy gave out her business cards during that long-ago hike at White Tanks.

"Thanks! I'll call her later. Right now, I've got to pick up my car and get to the hospital." She grabbed her bag and opened the door. Hot air from the outside swept into the cool car.

"Wait," he said.

"Yes?" She had developed an attachment for the three-letter word.

"I came by your office for a reason."

This could be the confrontation. "Yes," she said, wary now. She stepped out of the car, a hand on the open door, ready to shut it.

"I think I've figured out why you didn't show up for our dinner date on Sunday."

"Tell me." Anger seeped into her words. She was out of his car. She decided she could express herself. "Tell me what you've figured out."

"It has to do with that online dating site, *Love After Loss*, isn't it?"

So, he is admitting it.

"Yes. I saw your name and the photograph. How could you do that?"

"Do what?" For the first time since she'd met him, he raised his voice.

"Why this pretense?"

"What pretense? I don't understand what you're upset about." He closed his eyes and gripped the steering wheel tighter. The moment fibrillated. "You take one step forward and then move two steps back. You need to figure out what it is you want."

Silence. Muscles twitching, she clenched her hand on the car door.

This is a good moment to slam it shut.

"This is not a good time," he said. "But let me tell you this. If you want to get in touch, you know how to find me."

She shut the car door softly.

He didn't say good-bye. He didn't wave. He didn't look at her.

He simply drove off.

She rubbed her cheek. It stung as if he smote her with the back of his hand.

24

Lonely Car

August 3, 2012

Usha couldn't ruminate upon Arjay's cryptic statements. She sped to the hospital and rushed into Emergency. She found Veena ready to leave.

"They saw you already? Oh, no! I missed it."

"They said they'd make it quick, and they did. Let's go."

Is Veena trying to pile on the guilt?

Usha submerged the thought. She pointed to her daughter's wrist. "What did the doctor say?"

"It's nothing. Let's go."

Veena chose to be uncommunicative. In the car, she yanked out her phone and tapped out messages.

"What did they say?"

Veena answered without taking her fingers off the phone. "Just a contusion. The doctor told me I should take Ibuprofen if the pain got too much. My wrist is sprained, that's all." She lapsed into a sulk.

Sorting thoughts, Usha drove home through the rush hour traffic. Veena blamed her for the missed appointment and for everything else. Usha opened her mouth to remind her daughter the accident interfered with her schedule, not the hospital visit, and then changed her mind.

"Did the insurance agent call you?" she asked.

"Yes. But I was with the doctor so I have to call him back." Again, that subtle hint. Because of her mother, she'd missed talking to the insurance agent.

"So, call him now."

"Well, he's gone for the day. I have to call the toll-free number when I get home. They'll answer day or night. How come this Arjay Wheeler person showed up with you?"

The abrupt changed in topic confounded Usha. She wished her daughter would stay angry about her emergency room visit. It occurred to her that Veena might think Arjay and she were special friends.

Oh, Marcy, what have you shared with Veena?

Special friends, a term Usha coined. When a boy's name came up in conversation more than three times, Usha would ask the then high-school student Veena if he was a special friend. Those were the days when the boyfriend concept proved difficult for both Usha and Raja.

Usha forced a bantering tone. "What's with the questioning? This is hardly a legal matter."

The issue came to a halt, fortuitously, as Veena's phone rang. She became involved in an intense conversation. Not for the first time, Usha marveled at her daughter's ability to focus and multitask. The caller's employer had fired him unfairly and he hoped to find legal representation.

When Usha pulled into the two-car garage, the sight of Raja's seven-year-old sedan gave her an odd pang. She peeked in through the window. Raja's sunglasses nestled on the visor where he'd last tucked them. She decided they could stay there; they had for the past three years.

Veena hung up the phone as they got into the house.

"I'm sure insurance covers a rental until they decide whether to fix yours."

"It's too much bother to get a rental. I'll take Dad's car."

She spoke as if he were still around. Usha felt a pinch in her chest.

It didn't make economic sense, but she paid the insurance on the car and took care of maintenance. She told herself a second vehicle meant safety, giving the impression more than one person lived in the house. The automobile could be handy if hers went in for extended repairs. They were all excuses. The fact remained: she couldn't bring herself to sell his car.

Perhaps his car waited for such a situation, to provide Veena with transportation.

Raja's car key hung in the key holder, a series of hooks on the kitchen wall. She removed the key from his designated spot, second from left. Again, an odd sense of separation as she handed over the key ring.

She asked, "So what would you like for dinner? I can put a pizza in the oven. Or I can make some fried rice."

Choices. "Peanut butter and jelly sandwiches or grilled cheese sandwiches?" she'd ask five-year-old Veena. "Orange juice or apple juice?" Raja may have exerted his decision-making power, yet Veena chose. She chose to go back into first grade when Raja pushed her into second, she chose to stop playing tennis, she chose to study at an in-state university, and she chose to become a lawyer.

"Nothing," she replied now, her attention on a text message.

Usha wished Veena would be less distracted.

"Nothing?"

Veena grimaced as her right wrist accidentally hit the table's edge.

"I think you should take some medication."

"No, I'm fine. I'll pick it up later if I need it."

"You're not thinking of leaving now, are you?"

"I have to get back to the office."

"Now? It's late. You can go tomorrow."

"I have to go."

She'd retreated into the uncommunicative mode again.

Why the great hurry to leave?

"How can you drive? Your wrist?"

"See?" Veena held her hand up. She drew circles with her fingers, displaying mobility.

When Veena made up her mind, no argument worked. Usha kissed her daughter good-bye and told her to take care. She watched as Veena backed her father's automobile out of the garage.

Her car looked particularly lonely as she brought the garage door down. She couldn't remember a time when Raja's vehicle hadn't occupied their garage.

25

Liberation

August 3, 2012

Usha warmed a slice of pizza for her dinner. She sat at the kitchen table for forty minutes, cutting up her meal into minute bits, chewing each piece over and over again. A dessert might have gone down easier. Thoughts of Raja's tan sedan impeded. Before this model, he'd driven another tan one.

Long ago, he chose to park on the left. On his side of the garage, a tennis ball hung on a string from a hook in the ceiling. When his windshield hit the orb, he turned off the engine, his positioning perfect every time. Now the ball hung, desolate. She should cut that string.

Instinct told her his car wouldn't return to its spot. Veena would keep her father's vehicle and take the cash from the insurance company. She should park in the center to avoid the vacancy on one side of the garage. There would be no need to inch forward carefully any-more, no need to worry about scratching the paint on his car.

Her eye caught Raja's vacant slot in the key holder, second from the left. A sense of emptiness engulfed, as if a family member had gone for good, again. She rummaged through the kitchen drawer where she stored spares, found Raja's second key, and placed it in the empty hook.

The nagging did not ease its clutch. She pressed her fingers in cir-cular movements into her temples.

She powered on her computer and logged into *Begin Anew*. On that day with the swirling dust storm—it seemed so long ago now—when she'd locked herself in the bathroom, she'd been frantic, vulner-able, and apprehensive: wrong reasons to register on an online dating website.

Ignoring the blinking messages on the right-hand corner, she clicked on the "chat" icon. A representative immediately came on, asking how he might help. Disengagement, she found, was more difficult than registering. She convinced the representative she'd found a special someone and therefore needed to cancel the member-ship. He expressed delight and offered congratulations.

There, that is done. Or rather, undone.

Not quite, a voice reminded. Veena registered her on *Love After Loss*. If Usha had listed herself on it, her daughter would have said, "What a cheesy sounding name!"

A sharp twinge arced through her chest.

Why did Veena choose to sign me up? Things may have evolved different-ly with Arjay otherwise.

They might have continued their fledgling relationship. They might have discovered further areas of commonality. She might have found things about him to dislike. After all, she knew familiarity revealed flaws and manifested the unnoticed.

*Fact remains: he does have his profile on the site. He may yet meet some-
one, may have already.*

She looked for the scrap of paper with the information she needed.
She'd thrown it, hoping it would carry away the betrayal. Veena had
given her the password and login information twice. Once, on a lined
sheet that said "Notes" on the top. The second time on torn frag-
ment.

Usha looked through the drawers in the kitchen. She turned her
handbag upside down. Her moves became rapid, as if she had a
deadline.

I can call Veena. No. I am not ready to answer questions.

She closed her eyes. That awful moment when she recognized
Arjay's profile replayed. She filled a glass with water and took a long
swallow.

It can't be in the blue bathroom.

Illogical perhaps, yet she couldn't forestall a roll of anxiety every
time she thought of the bathroom and its locked door.

It has to be in my bedroom.

She lifted the sheets off her bed. No scrap of paper.

The master bathroom, then?

She couldn't locate it by the sink or on the floor. She turned the
trash can upside down. Strands of dark hair, balled up tissues, old
receipts, used-up lip gloss, an empty shampoo bottle, and bits of bar
soap cascaded to the floor. Stuck at the bottom of the can, she found
the log-in details.

As soon as she entered the web address, the dating site's claim-to-
fame twinkled in bright blue: *Love After Loss—The Number One Dating
Website for a Fulfilling Second Relationship!* She understood why Veena
chose this site.

The "Messages" link flashed green at the top right. Deciding to
ignore it, she clicked on the chat icon. A line popped up: *Someone will*

be with you shortly. Thank you for waiting. She typed "Hi" in the box and waited. And waited.

The green "Messages" light blinked, summoned. Arjay's statement haunted: "I didn't do anything."

Thoughts tussled.

He was a gentleman today. A mask? Is he trying to play nice? He may be trying to get back into my good books. Never mind. In a few more minutes, I will revoke the membership.

The message light vied for attention.

A vision rose of men in suits, standing in a line, competing for her notice. Just like the *swayamvaras* she had read about in her high school Indian History class.

In ancient India, she learned in that class, women had chosen their husbands in a practice called the *swayamvara*: *swayam* meaning self and *vara* meaning bridegroom. Suitors presented themselves at the ceremony where the bride chose one of them for her husband.

The Indian epic, *Ramayana*, tells the tale of Sita, the wife of Rama, who'd married him in a *swayamvara*.

Usha also read the romantic story of Princess Samyukta. The princess fell in love with King Prithviraj whom her father did not approve of. Her father arranged a *swayamvara* for her, inviting the most eligible of men. To insult Prithviraj, he erected a statue of him. At the *swayamvara*, defiant Samyukta garlanded the statue. Hidden behind the statue, Prithviraj manifested himself, gathered her up on to his horse, and rode away.

Usha slapped her forehead to bring herself back to reality. This was the age of technology; there were no romantic suitors on horses.

Three times. Three times, Arjay invited her, and three times, she accepted. He invited her to tour his school; she went and had lunch with him. She attended his open house. Marcy accompanied her— and technically, he called it a party, not a date—but she accepted.

Then, there was that dinner date.

She made him endure embarrassment.

She interlocked her fingers, placing her hands on her eyes. Raja should say something now. He didn't.

He'd gone silent.

The chat box came alive with a clink and jostled her out of pondering. "How can I help you?"

She went through a repeat of the *Begin Anew* scenario: the questions, the answers. The customer service personnel at all the dating sites received similar training, she decided. When she told the service agent she'd found someone, he wanted to know if it was through their site or through other social connections.

She settled on the partial truth. "I met someone at a coffee place."

⟡

The cell phone rang, scuttling her thoughts. She couldn't tell where the sound came from. The phone was not visible around the kitchen; she couldn't locate it on the table or the countertops. Rapidly, she opened drawers. She found the instrument among the spare keys.

"Do you ever pick up the phone? Do you even look at messages? I've been frantic! Finally, I caught Veena and she updated me. Are you home?" Marcy didn't waste time on preliminaries.

Usha heard Marcy's words spill and felt her throat constrict. She swallowed. "Yes, I'm home. Sorry, sorry. It's been a crazy day. I had to take my car in to the dealership, they took too long. So, I left it there and came back to work. Arjay came into the office; Veena had the accident. We went to the hospital, came home, and she took Raja's car... and..." Usha didn't halt the tears. She sniffed.

"Whoa... slow down, girl! You made no sense there. Calm

down. I know Veena's okay. That's the important thing."

A sob escaped.

"I'm coming tomorrow. I can't allow you to deal with all of this on your own."

Marcy, the dear soul.

"Don't."

"Why not? Are you telling me I shouldn't see my dear friend?"

Usha smiled through her tears. "Seriously, I'm okay. I have to catch up on work tomorrow anyway."

"What's wrong with the two of you? Veena said she's at work. A young girl working on a Friday evening? Something's wrong with that picture."

Usha found her way to the living room couch. She adjusted a decorative pillow on the couch to cushion her back. "Marcy, she is an adult."

"Are you sure you don't need me?"

Now, Marcy needs reassurance?

Usha stretched her legs out. She imagined Marcy at the other end, head cocked to one side, a hand pulling at her ear. "I'll always need you. There's a reason I don't want you to come."

"What?"

"I'm coming to see you next weekend." Usha pulled her knees up to her chest.

The declaration feels good. Liberating even.

She'd been so wrapped up in her own life, she hadn't visited Marcy once.

Time for change, perhaps.

Her friend let out a delighted whoop.

"I think I should check out your David," Usha said.

"Yes, of course. Not to change subjects, but tell me about the accident. When Arjay called, I went crazy. Couldn't believe it. He told me Veena was okay, but I still needed to hear from you."

Marcy did not remain silent about Arjay.

"Yes, he happened to be in my office, meeting a student, when the crash happened. I didn't know he'd called you."

"That was nice of him. Don't you think so?"

"Yes." Usha knew Marcy waited for more. She needed to change the topic. "So, I'll book my tickets and send you the confirmation."

"Oooh! I can't wait. Lots of talking to do! And we'll do such fun things while you're here."

When the landline rang, the house lay in darkness except for the kitchen light which stayed on, day or night, since Raja died. Usha's first thought, as always: *Veena!*

Heart catapulting into her mouth, she charged to the kitchen to pick up the phone. "What happened?"

"Are you asleep?" Veena asked.

"Of course. It's the middle of the night."

"Check your clock… it's only 9:30. But I can call later. You go back to sleep."

Usha blinked and looked at the clock on the microwave oven. Half past nine, just as Veena indicated.

I must have fallen asleep on the couch after speaking to Marcy.

She filled a glass with water from the faucet. "Did you call for a reason?" she asked Veena.

"No…"

Usha thought the negative did not sound too firm. Sometimes, Veena needed prodding. "Sure?"

"Yes. It can wait."

"Make up your mind." Usha thought Veena had grown out of

this phase a while ago. "Is it a 'yes' or a 'no?' In any case, I'm awake now, so you might as well tell me."

"Maybe this is not the right time."

"Why do you need the right time?" Warning bells tinkled in Usha's head.

"Oh, it's nothing." Veena's voice remained hesitant.

"Come on. You're annoying me. What is it?"

Is there a problem with Raja's car? Or worse, Veena's wrist? Is she hurt in other places? Perhaps she needs to go back to the hospital.

"If it's something I should know about, don't hesitate." The mother in Usha knew Veena brimmed with a confession.

"Well, well… I don't quite know how to tell you this. It's about *Love After Loss*."

"Hold on. Hold on right there. That story is over. I've canceled the membership."

"What?" Veena's voice grew louder.

"I told you, I'm not interested."

"But what about Arjay Wheeler?"

Bewildered, Usha gulped twice before she said, "What about him?"

Does Veena connect him with Love After Loss? *Or is she just asking about him as another potential date? Didn't Veena say she is calling about something else?*

"How come he was with you today?" Veena asked.

Perhaps this call is not about something else.

"I told you already. He was at our office, meeting a student, when you called. And, anyway, he doesn't really matter."

"He doesn't? Really?" Veena began to sound like a lawyer.

"Yes. He does not matter."

"Well, I guess I was worrying for no reason. So I can relax and stop feeling like a child who's been naughty."

"Naughty. Naughty? What did you do, Veena?" Her daughter might sound relaxed now, but Usha knew there had to be more.

"Nothing. It's of no consequence now that you've removed yourself from the dating site." Veena paused. "Or maybe it does matter. I don't know. Oh, I was only trying to help you."

"You've done enough by registering me on that site. Please don't do anything like that again."

"I won't. I promise."

"So, again, what did you do?" Usha knew something remained unsaid.

"Well, I kept asking and asking and asking you to check your messages on the site. There was one from a man called Arjay Wheeler." A throb of silence. "I responded," she whispered.

"What? Oh, my God!"

"No, no, no! Not for me. For you. And no, it wasn't some big love note. I just said, 'Thank you for expressing interest.' That's all. I didn't even sign the note. He'd have thought you sent him the note. I wanted to keep the ball rolling. You were taking too long."

Usha's head heated up like it would go up in flames. "Of all the things you've done..."

"But don't you see, he might have lost interest if I didn't send him a note or something. There are others on the site, too, you know."

Usha slapped her forehead and shouted, "I'm so mad, I cannot think straight. I am going to hang up before I lose it completely. So, goodnight. And don't even think of coming here. I need to be alone tonight."

26

Her Choice

August 4, 2012

Usha writhed in bed, struggling with the covering sheet as she heard Arjay say over and over again, "You know how to find me." Waves of heat streamed through her body. She threw off the sheet before turning the ceiling fan to the highest setting. Soon, a shiver started in her lower belly, and she covered herself with both a sheet and a blanket. "You need to figure out what it is you want," he'd said to her.

She woke at the faint light of dawn, made herself a cup of tea, and watched CNN. An hour later, the clock read 5:32 AM. She willed herself to return to bed, took her Kindle, hoping some reading could lull her to sleep. It didn't. She clenched her fists.

She wanted to call Veena. But her daughter wouldn't wake until much later. She itched to give Veena a piece of her mind. Of all the things she had done, sending Arjay the note was the most disappointing, the most embarrassing, and the most infuriating.

The dressing-down must wait. I may need to delay until Veena recovers from her injuries. Veena's swollen nose and injured wrist don't look good. The emergency room doctor had said she would be fine; still, one never knows. The swelling can get worse. She may need medication.

But all that does not absolve her.

Thoughts of the accident reminded her of Arjay's presence at the accident site.

Her thoughts deafened. She needed outside sound for balance.

That is the trouble with this house. It is too quiet.

She tuned her bedside radio to KJZZ, the local National Public Radio station, listened to *Morning Edition*. They spoke of promising economic numbers. They spoke of home sales inching up. They spoke of lower unemployment.

She jumped out of bed, strode through her bedroom to the living room and then through the dining area to the kitchen.

The problem with my housing situation: this place has grown too big for one person. How many rooms do I need? Not three bedrooms, a study, and three bathrooms.

She paused by the blue bathroom on her way to the kitchen. She saw the door closed and pushed it open without entering. Her rescuers had forced the door open, damaging the handle, which now hung crooked. She reflected for some moments and decided she should fix the door.

She felt an urge to go to the office. "It's Saturday. There's no need," she mumbled to herself. Still, the compulsion wouldn't go away. She tried to rationalize the urge. Work awaited her. So much back-log remained. She'd left in a tear yesterday, abandoning Arjay and Andres in the middle of a conversation. Arjay's half-finished bottle of water probably still sat on the meeting area table. And

Andres, the poor boy—she should send him a message and re-schedule his appointment.

Staying home will only mean more maudlin thoughts.

She succumbed to the urgency. With a renewed sense of purpose, she ate breakfast: a slice of toast and half a cup of yogurt.

Still only 8:00 A.M.

She made some Indian tea. It scalded her tongue. Instead of wait-ing for the tea to cool, she poured it into a travel mug and drank it on the way to work.

Arriving at the library by nine, she found a perfect parking spot under the shade of the solar panels. The sun shone in ferocity, but the air felt humid, as if heralding another monsoon storm. The hot tea made her sweat in the air-conditioned car.

In two months, the climate will be magnificent.

Usha wiped sweat off her neck and between her breasts with her handkerchief. In two months, Arizonans would forget about having endured the hot summer, get out of their houses, resume outdoor activities, and revel in the natural beauty of the state.

She threw the girls at Customer Service a smile and a greeting be-fore stepping into the glass elevators. The doors shut. Instead of punching the number for her floor, she took in the view. A child, about five, stood with his mother before the black-bottomed pool, clutching something in his fist. Screwing his eyes shut, he used his right arm to throw a coin into the pool.

Usha pressed the "Open" button on the panel, stepped out, and walked over to the pool. She rummaged in the bottom of her bag and located a shiny penny. After kissing the coin, she tossed it into the pool. Before it joined other relatives at the bottom, she heard a small splash.

Still early, the library employees hadn't quite settled down. Some enthusiastic library patrons, however, milled around, asking questions, searching among the shelves.

She let herself into her office and turned on the lights.

This place never fails to welcome me with its warmth and to comfort me. My second home: the library and this office.

A half-empty bottle of water sat on her desk. She drained it.

Arjay came into this office yesterday. Not for a confrontation.

As she went to throw her empty water bottle into the recycling bin, she paused by the meeting area. Only one bottle sat on the table.

Arjay's water remained on the table from yesterday. His chair, askew, spoke of the urgency with which they'd left. Sitting in the chair he'd occupied yesterday, she placed her empty bottle next to his and stared.

She rose and went back into her office. Patricia had left a couple of handwritten messages on her table.

Andres had also left her a note. "Thank you for introducing me to Dr. Wheeler. I have his card and I'm going to meet him at his office next week. He said he will help me with my admission. Thank you!"

Nice boy. My job is done for now. Arjay has said he will help him.

She hadn't turned off her computer when she left yesterday. Twenty email messages greeted her. No message from Arjay.

Veena might have called to see if she remained furious. When she checked, she found no messages, no calls. Not from Veena. Not from Arjay.

She tossed Patricia's messages into her drawer along with the note from Andres.

"You know how to find me." Arjay's voice echoed in her mind again. She tried to suppress it by pushing the disorder on her table to one side.

She attempted to bring some organization to the clutter on her table and noticed that the table's surface needed dusting. Grabbing a paper towel, she began to swipe at the dust.

As far as the whole dating experiment went, she'd reached the end of the road. Which meant she would not see Arjay again. Ever. A dull thud marked time in her chest.

Concentrate. Keep your attention on the task at hand.

The next item in her hand—*College Essays That Make a Difference.*

How long has it been here? Two weeks?

Only two weeks ago, she'd met Joel upstairs.

How could the people at the dating site have decided I have anything in common with that awful man?

A smile escaped as she recalled her frenetic escape into her office with the book in her hands.

The smile disappeared.

Arjay had knocked. He found her office. A conversation followed, his words hesitant—a departure from their first meeting. She rubbed her forehead and tried to reconstruct the dialog.

What did he say?

She remembered thinking he came across as strange.

"Before we start… So, you know about me?" That was the strange question.

But he told me all about himself the previous Saturday at the coffee shop.

"Yes, of course," she had answered.

Their conversation crisscrossing, but not connecting. He assumed she knew about him from *Love After Loss.* "I'm new at this… whole thing."

He'd been talking about online dating. She assumed it was the new job in college admissions.

And my confident response?

"I know. It's daunting isn't it?"

She crossed her arms on her desk.

At what point did he find me on the website?

It had to be after their meeting in the library, after their conversation at the coffee shop.

"Raja," she pleaded, "Can you help me?"

He hadn't spoken to her in a while and he didn't dial in now.

His absent voice told her it was her choice. This time, it was her choice alone.

She studied the book that had been on her desk for over two weeks. Perhaps the librarians had already logged it in as "Missing" or "Lost" on the system. Making a determination, she picked up the book and took the stairs up to the fifth floor two at a time and hurried toward the stacks in the back.

Thoughts quickened with her pace. Today's date: August 4, 2012. Only three weeks ago, on this floor, she'd met Arjay for the first time. So much had happened since then. He'd come into her office, invited her to his university where they had lunch. Then, they'd run into each other when she went hiking with Marcy. He'd invited her to his house and given her a gift, a basket of vegetables from his garden.

She hadn't used the vegetables yet.

It will distress me to see them rot.

She considered the dinner date disaster for which she hadn't apologized.

My behavior nothing short of callous, unfeeling.

Despite which, he helped out with Veena's crisis—the accident.

Mistaken identity or not, instinct connected them. He'd called it their "synchrony." She'd enjoyed the ease of his company, the conversation, his quiet presence. They'd spoken for three hours at the coffee shop. At the end, a curious sense of continuity, his hand on her back as he ushered her out the door in a gesture of unexpected familiarity.

She'd memorized his attractive, crooked smile, the neat goatee, his lean, athletic body. Other stored details in her consciousness: the khaki shorts and the navy shirt, the bits of paper sticking out of the books tucked under his left arm.

Thoughts tumbled like clothes in a dryer. She closed her eyes, pictured him at her favorite spot: the table on the north side with the unparalleled view of the mountains in the distance, the *METRO* rail running on Central, and the Phoenix Art Museum at the corner.

If she looked out the window from her vantage point on the fifth floor, she should be able to see their coffee shop. The label fit: "*their* coffee shop."

With her head down, she collided into a man with a stack of books. The top three thudded to the floor. This time her foot was not injured.

"Well, well, well... Is this déjà vu or what? Making a habit of this?"

The young man she'd crashed into three weeks ago grinned. But for him, she might have missed meeting Arjay that first time.

"Sorry, so sorry," she said.

"I'm just kidding," he laughed. "Don't worry. You seem to be in a hurry. Just go."

She bent down to get the books. "Let me pick these up for you. Sorry again!" She beamed as she handed them to him. Throwing, "Have a great weekend," behind her, she dashed to the north side of the fifth floor. She felt his smile warm her back.

Her soul knew.

She recognized Arjay's head, the width of his shoulders, and the curl of hair on his collar. He sat at her table, looking out of the window. She took three deep breaths and slowed down. When she reached him, she placed a tentative hand on his right shoulder. He didn't turn around.

"You knew where to find me," he said. Her ears picked up a lilt in his voice. "What took you so long? I've been waiting here for thirty minutes. Come here, I want to show you something."

He stood, still looking out through the window. When she went to stand by him, he draped an arm across her shoulders and hugged her to his side. As if it was the most natural thing in the world, she wound her arm around him in response.

"I'm sorry," she said, "for more than the wait. There's so much I have to say."

"All that can wait. Can you see it?" he asked, pointing. "There's our coffee shop. Could I interest you in a cup of coffee or maybe an iced drink?"

About the Author

Sudha Balagopal's fiction straddles continents, melding cultures and blending thoughts, representing ideas and desires from the east and the west. Her work delves into the everyday lives of ordinary people to reveal larger, universal truths. She is the author of two short story collections, *There are Seven Notes* and *Missing and Other Stories*. When she's not writing, Sudha teaches yoga.

Connect with Sudha at SudhaBalagopal.com and find her on Facebook.

Other Works by Sudha Balagopal:

There are Seven Notes
Missing and Other Stories